Margaret J. Carr

KILL ME FOR A THIRD TIME

A Sophie Curtiss Mystery
The Untold Story

Paul W. J. Carr © 2022

The book is a crime mystery and a work of fiction. If any of the content resembles a real person or any actual events, it is a pure coincidence.

However, please note, no animals or humans were harmed in its writing.

He only just remembered in time not to swear when the text pinged on his phone.

He hadn't expected anyone to disturb his family time and he'd only just held his tongue in time. Gemma would have objected if he'd cussed in front of the children, she was a stickler for formality although, had the children been in bed, she would have used language which matched any of his profanities.

It was family time and along with Gemma and their two young kids, he was seated in the specially converted home cinema in their sumptuous home. His wife on the deeply cushioned chair, with her legs curled under her, was concentrating on her pedicure while he sat, cosily between the six- and four-year-olds. They were watching the same film, The Gruffalo, they must have watched five or six times before, but it was the children's current favourite.

Jake Morgan released his right arm from around the little girl's shoulders.

'Aw, Daddy,' she was such a little sweetie, and he kissed the top of her fair head. Son Aaron's attention was glued to the screen, and he hardly noticed, but out of the corner of his eye, he'd seen Gemma silently roll her eyes in annoyance at this intrusion. He ignored her, instead concentrating on his daughter's disappointment.

'Sorry Princess,' he said, standing and grabbing his errant mobile. 'Daddy'll just take this outside, then I'll be right back.'

The text had come from Clarke, and it was obvious he was panicking, so it was best to put him straight, before he blabbed to the wrong people.

Morgan let himself out through the garage and into the front garden. The evening was as black as pitch, the moon well hidden behind a thick bank of clouds. He'd cautiously switched off the outside security light, which patrolled this area of his property, lest it would attract attention. Attention was something he avoided at all costs.

'Well,' he sounded annoyed, as he faced the man who had suddenly appeared from behind one of the carefully sculpted bushes. 'What is it, Lyall? This had better be good. You are disturbing a film evening with my family.'

Lyall Clarke looked nervous, and his eyes darted from side to side, then at the man who looked and sounded every bit the successful businessman he portrayed to the world.

'I've got info that the police know about next month's shipment and are planning to intercept the ship before it gets here. They'll be waiting for us.'

'I know.' Morgan hardly reacted, in fact he sounded very calm.

Clarke blinked.

'You knew already? I don't get it. How could you know?'

'Because I have, let's say 'a friend' in the force, who is keeping me up to date. He's reliable, always has been in the past.'

Clarke was at a loss how to respond and couldn't think straight. Jake seemed so calm, so unconcerned and perhaps this deal didn't mean as much to a man already worth millions, as it did to him. This unexpected 'spanner in the works' could mean the end of all Kyall's plans for the future and he was getting too old for this game. He knew full well that sooner or later he'd be back inside, and this time for a very long stretch.

He'd already made up his mind if the Boss pulled it off, he'd take his cut, a substantial and life changing amount and move abroad, and disappear to the Bahamas.

Of course, his girlfriend had to be in on his plans. She was happy to live abroad, just as long as he had a healthy bank account to fund her extravagant lifestyle, and Kyall quite fancied an easy retirement of sun, sea, and drinks on the beach.

But a future of luxury had all rested on the Boss and the lads being able to pull off this lucrative deal but if the law had found out, then their future was 'screwed'.

There was complete silence for a few minutes and although he couldn't see his boss's face, he sensed Morgan was in control and unconcerned. He had always relied on Jake and for his part, after Clarke had helped solve a personal problem some years previously, he'd kept his promise.

However, Kyall stayed quiet waiting for Morgan to speak, he had a temper, and it was wise not to provoke him. When Morgan next spoke it was sharp, clipped.

'We go ahead as planned. We'll not fail when we've come this close.' the man continued thoughtfully.

'We still have weeks to go, and we can still save this. I already have a way to do that.'

He sounded overly confident, and Clarke relaxed his stressed shoulders. He could always rely on Jake.

'What d'you want me to do?'

'I don't want you or the others to do anything, yet.'

He paused, obviously working things out in his head and the man at his side knew better than to interrupt.

'Give me a few days to sort out something and get everything in place. I'll be in touch in a day or two.'

Clarke felt the warm breath, tinged with a hint of lager and very expensive after shave, on his face. An indication Jake had moved closer to make sure his next statement was understood and carried out.

'Now, don't ever come to my house again unless you've been invited.'

Clarke knew that would never happen; the two men normally moved in vastly different circles.

'I'll text you a message on a pay-as-u-go phone when I'm ready, and I've made the necessary adjustments to the plan. Understood?'

Kyall nodded although Morgan couldn't have seen it.

'Understood Jake,' he answered.

Chapter 1

Sophie now had all this time on her hands, something that was out of cinque with her former busy life of running the home, caring for her family, and writing her column for the local newspaper. All that had irreversibly changed, and she missed the old uniformity of her days.

It had been a terrible year for the entire family after Sophie had started with the blinding headaches, then the diagnosis and the months of treatment.

Richard had taken compassionate leave to be there at her side, but it was ten-year-old Kirstie who had worried and suffered the most, not fully understanding her mother's sickness. Their daughter's personality, usually so happy-go-lucky, had changed and as the weeks had turned into months, she'd grown resentful, blaming everyone, and Sophie in particular, for being ill. Kirstie was hitting out, not just at Sophie but at everyone.

That was except for Richard, feeling she and her father were being punished for something she didn't understand.

Once her mother had been given the all clear by the specialist, it was hoped Kirstie would become her old self again, yet even as her mother slowly recovered back to full health, it was taking longer for the child to come to terms. Instead, she had grown more remote, moody, and argumentative. Her school grades suffered, and the teachers were concerned.

It had been Sophie's sister, Helen who had suggested Mum, Dad and Kirstie should go and spend the summer holidays in Arizona. There, Kirstie would have the space to run wild, the horses, her cousins, and a chance to return to being a child again.

Since they'd flown out a fortnight before, Sophie had Skyped with her parents and her daughter every couple of days. She missed Kirstie more than she could have imagined and looked forward to the days she could talk to her over in the States, albeit by a screen.

Of course, this didn't always work out as she hoped. They had to gauge it right and not forget the time difference, and as Kirstie was more often than not out somewhere on the vast ranch with her cousins, she was not always available to chat to her mother back home.

'Never mind,' Sophie would try not to look or sound too hurt, when her mother was explaining yet again Kirstie was doing something else.

'At least my daughter is having fun and acting like a ten-year-old should, after the trauma and worry of the past year.'

Why could she never throw off this feeling of guilt, as if it had all been her fault?

She'd have liked to return to her old job and at first, the editor on the paper had been very understanding.

'You'll always have a place on the Advertiser once you feel up to coming back, Sophie,' Ellie Roberts had said, the latest in a line of new, young, fresh, editors, who over the years had replaced her first boss, Bill Howarth.

It had not quite worked out that way.

With numerous excuses from Ms Roberts as to why it wasn't going to happen, not yet, Sophie had finally accepted she was considered redundant, an old-school journalist and when the 'just-out-of-university' Merry Graham took over her column, then the writing was very much on the wall.

Sophie's husband was working longer hours, it could often be days before Richard could nip home for any longer than a hurried meal and a short nap, so the couple seemed to be growing further apart, their marriage strained.

With all these empty hours and days to fill, she caught up with books she'd always intended to read or watched hour after hour of mind-numbing day-time TV. But even as she recuperated back to full health, Sophie was bored with little to occupy her days,

'Why not take up a hobby?' her dad had suggested.

'Try something creative,' her doctor had suggested. 'Your brain might be healed, but maybe your mental health could do with help from some form of a calming activity?'

So, Sophie took their advice and, on a whim, joined the local amateur watercolour classes.

Although with almost no artist ability, she found she quite enjoyed the easy and uncomplicated twice weekly sessions. Her still life pictures and landscapes resembled a colourful collection of blobs and streaks.

'Art is subjective,' said Bob, the patient teacher. 'Your work could easily sit next to any of the impressionist and modernist painters.' He encouraged, but Sophie wasn't convinced.

She studied her latest painting of what should have been a floral display, but resembled an explosion in a paint store, from every angle. 'It's very colourful,' Bob said enthusiastically.

He was just being kind; anyone could see that!

However, she was enjoying this new experience and started to look forward to each session, especially since April had joined a month later.

April Cox, about the same age, recently divorced seemed a loner. At first, she was reluctant to talk about herself, didn't join in with the camaraderie and chatter from the rest of the group and just like Sophie, April was hopeless at putting paint to canvas and creating something like a picture.

The two bonded and it didn't matter that neither had a single artistic bone in their bodies and, regardless of their combined lack of talent, they enjoyed every minute.

It was during one of their after-class glasses of wine, at the bar around the corner to the college, that April suggested the holiday.

'We could rent somewhere on the coast and chill for a couple of weeks.'

Chapter 2

It had happened so fast: it was almost before Sophie had had time to think, when April had gone ahead with the arrangements.

'I suppose,' Sophie considered. 'She hadn't wanted me to be bothered with all the details, which was kind of her, but it would have been nice if I'd actually had a say.'

She inwardly sighed. Since her operation people's kindness from family, and friends, had at times been suffocating. She should not be so critical.

'April has gone to a lot of trouble setting this up and I should be grateful,' she silently rebuked, consciously relaxing against the comfortable passenger's seat and taking in the changing scenery.

April had used her car to drive them to this part of the coast. Sophie knew she should be able to recognise some of the villages and towns they'd passed through but, since her illness, she found her sense of direction wasn't as clear as it once had been.

'We've arrived,' April stated as they'd been driving over the brow of a hill, and the panorama suddenly opened out before them.

The crescent shaped coastline, quite rugged in places, was dotted with small shallow inlets and coves and in the far distance to the north, the shadowy outlines of hills and mountains, gave it an other-worldly sense. She smiled to herself imagining Kirstie would have likened the distance vista to her current favourite film franchise, The Lord of the Rings. This might not be as others saw it, but then Kirstie's vivid and often outrageous imagination was even better than her own. The thought of her daughter and her parents overseas and Richard back home made her feel suddenly bereft, and not for the first time she was missing her family and doubting their distance.

As she gazed out over the sea to the horizon, the sun was making its majestic way across the sky to the west, and to meet the line of clouds set ready for a spectacular sunset in another five or six hours.

Sophie let her mind drift, she was here to rest and rest she would — and paint. She was already visualising her first attempt of a fantasy landscape of misty blues, and vibrant aqua tones against the backdrop of muted browns and ochres of sand and rocks. The perfect scene was given an extra 'chocolate box feel' by a crude wooden fishing jetty jutting out into the gentle lapping water. All that was missing was a young boy, fishing line in hand dangling his bare feet over the edge, or a gnarled old fisherman with his bait box at his side. This scene was empty and lacking, and from nowhere she had a sudden rush of homesickness and loss which made her gasp.

April didn't appear to have noticed Sophie's hesitation, but had stopped the car on the crest of the small hill, so they could take in the scenery set out before them.

'Isn't this perfect?' she asked.

'Yes it is,' Sophie answered. It was probably the long journey, but she felt, since they'd stopped for a comfort break and coffee mid-morning, she had grown more and more weary and seemed to lose track of where they were. This she put down to the medication she still had to take and dismissed it, she was looking forward to a painting holiday.

'It's quite isolated and private here,' continued April. 'So we shouldn't be overwhelmed by other holiday makers, but just wait 'til you see the house.'

The first sight of the modern property took Sophie's breath away. It was less a house and more a beautiful architecturally inspired work of art, which appeared as part of the hill, so that it became one with the landscape. As they drove down the narrow private road, and stopped, Sophie was able to get a better look at the building from the front. It faced the coast with a large glass balcony across the exterior, the whole, seamlessly blending back into the solid rock. Its impressive facade came somewhere between a TV's Kevin McCloud futuristic build and the filmed location situated amongst the statues of Mount Rushmore in the iconic Hitchcock film, *North By Northwest.*

'When I show you the inside, you'll see that beyond the balcony which makes the most of the view, the sliding glass doors lead into a large lounge on two levels,' April sounded matter of fact and more than quoting a description from a publicity brochure. Sophie wondered if she'd stayed here before.

'You've holidayed here before?' she asked.

There was a pause as April stopped the car and parked before the partially hidden underground garage door. She didn't answer and the two, first collecting their wheelie luggage from the boot, stood at the large wooden door, positioned close to the garage. As if it was something she'd done before, April pinned in a number into the keypad on the wall at the side, and silently the door swung open.

'It's all hi-tech security,' she explained as if it was necessary. 'Only specific six-digit numbers open one or two doors, so no need for keys.

It was as if she suddenly remembered Sophie's earlier question. 'I've been once before just after it finished being built,' she didn't elaborate more and ended on a light note and with a knowing wink.

'Believe me, there was a ton of money spent on it.'

She concentrated on dragging her bag into a large, square space with doors on the three sides. Central to this space was a staircase, constructed of glass and wrought iron which disappeared to a lower level.

'It's an upside-down house, so down there are three bedrooms and their en-suites.'

It seemed that was the extent of her explanation, at least for the moment.

'I think a cup of tea is the first thing we need after that drive.'

Without hesitating she opened the correct door and Sophie followed.

As expected, it was ultra-modern and well stocked with appliances and white goods. April opened a cupboard and then seemed to know which door hid the fridge freezer.

'That's good. They have been stocked already.'

Who 'they' were, whoever it was had performed that particular domestic task she didn't add, and as soon as the kettle was filled and switched on, April led Sophie back into the hallway.

She opened another door and waited for her companion to go inside.

'The magnificent lounge and balcony,' she said, standing back so her companion could take in everything. 'It was designed so anyone in this room or out through there on the balcony can appreciate the full view.' She sounded more like a travel agent, and Sophie nodded her appreciation as she stepped onto the cool laminated floor.

The rectangle shaped room, the minimal space was bright with shimmering waves of light bouncing off the pure white walls and the white leather of the low-slung sofa's set at different angles so anyone seated could gaze out through the food to ceiling glass bi-fold doors.

April stayed silent, waiting while Sophie took in everything and seemingly delighted when Sophie made the appropriate sounds of delight, as if she'd been showing off her own home.

Once again in the hall April pointed at the final closed door, dismissing it with: 'Oh that's just the wine cellar and more storage.' She made no effort to show this to Sophie but, as if she'd already mentioned the fact, she said brightly. 'Like I told you. This place belongs to a friend, and he said we could stay here for a fortnight, rent free.'

Sophie was still not used to coping with her temporary memory lapse, her specialist had warned her of that but assured her over time it would fade, but she was pretty sure April had never mentioned about the place being owned by a friend. She was sure she'd have remembered that. Had she misunderstood from the start and assumed it was a rented holiday cottage close to the sea? Was it April's surprise for her new friend? Maybe? Sophie wasn't sure and decided to let it go after all, it wouldn't be the first time her brain played tricks on her memory these days.

Chapter 3

Sophie rested against the canvas back of her seat and considered her picture on the easel from differing angles. It may not be a Botticelli, but it wasn't too bad. It was colourful, in bright blues, green, reds, yellow, in fact the full spectrum of the rainbow. An abstract, an interpretation but not necessarily a true representative of the scene before her.

That didn't matter. It was restful and enjoyable spending time daubing watercolour onto the paper, and spending even more time gazing out to sea or turning towards the misty hills in the far distance. To her left with a good space between them, April sat in a director's chair concentrating on her own masterpiece. Neither spoke, their words would have been lost and they'd chat later comparing notes and analysing their paintings, over a pleasant meal and a glass of wine.

Now as the sun rose to its zenith and the wisps of clouds drifted across the sky, Sophie adjusted her enormous hat, so it not only protected her face but bare shoulders. She removed her sunglasses to check more on her choice of colour for the distant bank of mountains. If she could just give an impression of their strength and permanency with a few splashes of pale to mid-grey against the paler blue background, then she might have it about right.

Sophie smiled to herself. Even better if she turned the whole image upside down and let the very watery, water colours run, drip and blend into one another. Perfect! Just the result she was aiming for.

She left her 'latest masterpiece' on the easel to dry, and let her gaze drift around the bay enjoying the gentle sweep of the land framing the mass of water and the distant hills and mountains she'd been at pains to get right in her painting. There was no doubt even after a couple of days she was feeling more relaxed and the murmurs of pain across the top of her head that sometimes affected her vision was diminishing, as she'd been told it would.

'Give it time,' the specialist had said. 'You had major surgery and you will feel discomfort for a while as the brain heals itself.' It did feel as if the peace and quiet of this ideal location was working its magic.

Overnight, or sometime while the women had been inside the villa, someone had left a small boat with an outboard motor, tethered to the wooden jetty, and had left it to rock gently in the swell. April hadn't mentioned this intruder, so maybe she hadn't seen it yet. She'd ask about it later.

Had they arrived to visit someone living close by, along this stretch of coast? But it was private land with no other buildings or signs of people for miles, so perhaps the boat had been abandoned? But what then had happened to the person or persons who had come this far? Sophie dwelt on the conundrum for only a matter of seconds before her thought dismissed it as irrelevant.

She welcomed the breeze cooling her bare limbs before reaching down to the large beach bag dumped in the sand at her feet and which sat beside the canvas holdall that she used for her painting paraphernalia. She found her mobile phone, dropped to the bottom, beneath an assortment of water bottle, suncream, tissues and a small hand fan.

She checked again just in case. There was still no signal, but it had become a habit, to check every now and then, although that had stayed the same from the first day. She thought she'd find the phone's charger in her bag, but perhaps she'd forgotten to pack it and as she couldn't use the phone, it seemed the missing charger was irrelevant.

'The forgetfulness is only a temporary thing,' she'd been told, but it was a worry not being able to remember even the simplest of things.

'It's impossible to get a mobile or internet signal here,' April had explained, sounding unconcerned at the prospect of not being able to contact anyone.

'And,' she'd continued unperturbed,' my friend never bothered to get a landline put in, as this was meant to be a retreat from the rigours of business.'

So once again April was referring to this mysterious owner without giving anything away.

'Just as well,' April had shrugged as if it was for Sophie's own good. 'What you need is complete rest, not being bothered with text or emails.'

It had been on the tip of Sophie's tongue to object to this arrangement, she did not like being completely cut off from Richard and her family, but maybe she could borrow April's car and drive to the nearest village, which her friend had said, was some distance away.

'Why would we need to go all that way when we have everything we need right here?' April had argued, and she was right when it came to food and everyday provisions. The cupboards and drawers were well stocked, and the huge freezer could have fed an army for a month.

But that didn't provide fresh fruit, salad, and vegetables and, importantly, no way to contact the outside world

None of this seemed to bother April. She seemed completely at ease with the arrangement, almost as if she welcomed the complete isolation.

Sophie, satisfied with her morning work. The upside-down picture of the sea and the sky and the beach, now drying in the heat, was looking quite presentable. Her best effort so far. She might even frame it and hang it on a wall back home, as a reminder of this painting holiday.

Using a hand to shield her eyes from the sun and the reflections bouncing off the calm water, she peered again at the lonely, abandoned motorboat. If it had been just left then, providing it was still in working order, maybe she could take it and sail along the coast to find civilization? A town or village, somewhere she could phone Richard and let him know she was well.

They'd not spoken since the morning she'd left and even then, his mind had been focusing on the days and weeks ahead when his team would be working alongside the NCA to arrest an international criminal gang. He'd not told her too much, but she knew it was on-going and would be taking up most of his days.

Then it might give her an opportunity to Skype Mum and Dad, and Kirstie. She missed them, in particular her daughter who, it has to be said, had been angry and insolent since Sophie's illness. The ten-year-old had blamed her mother for everything. For getting sick in the first place, having something wrong with her brain and nearly dying, as if it had all been her mother's fault. Kirstie was ten, a child, and the fact her mother might suddenly have died, she was, childlike, hitting out at the one person who would change her young life forever. Sophie understood, but it didn't make the mother/daughter relationship any easier.

If she could just get to talk to the people, she loved most of all instead of this feeling of helplessness?

Leaving her picture on the easel, she stood and wandered closer to her friend, who seemed completely wrapped up in studying, then transferring to her painting, a small outcrop of rocks to her left. These had been partially hidden from Sophie's angle of vision, further along the crescent, and she could now see they formed a particular, natural sculptural work of art in their own right. April was engrossed in getting the subject to her liking.

'That's pretty damn good,' she said lightly, appreciating that the image of the cubist style rocks, and shingle would not have been to her own creative temperament, nevertheless it was a decent representation.

April jumped, quite violently, as if Sophie had been a sudden threat.

'Oh Sophie,' she visually relaxed. 'Sorry I was miles away,' as if to justify her reaction she added, 'an artistic fugue.'

She studied her own canvas from different angles as if it was only now, she was looking at the finished work. 'Thanks. I'm really quite pleased with it myself.' She put aside her brush and stood leaving the canvas on the easel.

'Have you finished your picture?' she asked, barely glancing towards the other 'painting station'.

'I have,' answered Sophie.

'Good. Good,' but she seemed distracted, and Sophie didn't think it had anything to do with their paintings. April glanced at her man-sized wristwatch.

'Time for a spot of lunch,' she said, with a flick of a hand. 'If you could grab your art equipment, I'll leave mine here until later. Follow me and I'll go on ahead to prepare us some lunch.'

She didn't wait for an answer but leaving everything, she marched back towards the steps leading to the villa. April hadn't just seemed distracted, but her mood was of undisguised impatience, leaving Sophie a little confused by her distinctive change.

Sophie, thoughtfully, watched her go. She'd tackle later, if that was the right phrase, the subject of communicating with the outside world, something April didn't seem to be bothered with.

The top part of the building was just in sight, the glass sparkling and reflecting in the light and from this angle, a few yards from the steps, it appeared to hover, unconnected like a magical crystal palace, against the deep blue and cloudless sky.

As she collected together her painting kit, the easel, finished picture and bags, Sophie made up her mind. Over lunch she'd insist either she could borrow April's car, or they could go together, to the nearest town so she could phone or email Richard and her family in the States. In fact, a chance of a change of scenery, a chance to browse amongst any shops and to buy the odds and ends that were always missed when getting ready for a holiday. It was a reasonable request: after all she wasn't being held as a prisoner in the villa.

Chapter 4

April served out the last of the crisp salad into side dishes and then placed the pieces of grilled sole onto their plates. She had already poured out glasses of chilled white wine when Sophie had arrived back inside. Once she'd unloaded her burden, she joined her friend at the breakfast bar.

It was as they tucked into the delicious food, both surprisingly famished after a morning of painting, 'Perhaps after we've eaten, we could drive to a town or village,' she waited for April to agree or disagree, and it appeared April was considering her suggestion.

'I just think,' Sophie continued, as if she was having to argue or debate the option.

'We've not moved from here since we arrived. A change of scenery and a chance to stock up on perishable food, and maybe have a look round — and find somewhere to phone or text my husband?'

She paused. 'Just to let Richard and my family know I'm well and having a nice restful time.'

'That's a good idea,' her friend nodded and smiled. 'I'll drive so I'll not have another glass of wine, but you finish your glass.'

She was suddenly enthusiastic.

'Tell you what,' she glanced at the large contemporary clock on the wall. 'It's just on half twelve and, if I know village shops, they usually close for lunch, so it would be pointless going much before two,' April grinned across the breakfast bar at Sophie. 'So, I'll finish up here, it's only down to loading the dishwasher, while you have a rest on your bed for half an hour. I'll grab a shower and then read my book, until you are ready, then we could go out toward the nearest town and maybe have dinner while we're there. There's bound to be a half decent restaurant, or if not, a McDonald's or Colonel Sanders.'

Sophie nodded in agreement.

It didn't take much persuading these days to have a rest or short sleep, and she wandered off in the direction of her stairs leading down to the bedrooms. She could hear April clatter about the kitchen as she dropped down on the top cover of the king-size bed and yawned deeply. She seemed more exhausted than normal, but she had been warned she would have a few tiring days amongst the rest.

She sighed with anticipation, already looking forward to a drive out to somewhere new, and closed her eyes.

Sophie stirred. Something had woken her from a dreamless sleep. A sound, a noise, but then it could just have been the noise of a seagull outside her bedroom window.

For a millisecond she had trouble remembering where she was, fully expecting to find herself in her bedroom back home. But this wasn't the familiar room, decorated in shades of gentle mint green and cream she shared with Richard. This room was decorated in stark white, like some kind of luxury cell. Everything was white! From the walls to the furniture, to the rugs scattered across the expense of white

Carrera marble. The fierceness and starkness made her blink, and she recognised the murmur of a pain across the crown on her head. Sitting up she ran her fingers through her cropped hair, she'd always had long, dark hair but since her operation she'd kept the now salt and pepper locks short and manageable.

Of course, she was on holiday in this private villa in the middle of nowhere.

Her mind and thoughts seemed vague, and she struggled to concentrate on the here and now. Her body felt weak, her throat was dry, and she reached for the glass and jug of water, and one of her prescription painkillers in the packet, on the bedside table.

Suddenly she remembered. They'd arranged to go for a drive to find a town or village. How long had she been asleep?

The time on her wristwatch said she'd slept for over three hours!

'Oh Lord,' she swung her legs off the side of the bed, surprised at how leadened her legs felt. There was no sound from anywhere in the building, and she made her way out into the lower floor's vast hallway with the other doors all closed. In case April had followed her lead and was taking a nap, she knocked on her bedroom door, and with no answer, opened it a snick and peered inside. The room next to hers, was identical in furnishing, and empty of its occupant. Sophie barely glanced in the direction of the closed and locked door of the wine cellar opposite with the keypad on the wall used to get in. She'd not been inside or wasn't particularly interested if it seemed off limits. It appeared April, had been given permission to help herself and obviously had the pin number, so daily would go, and bring out a bottle of wine to accompany a meal.

Sophie thought she'd locate April in the lounge or out on the balcony, and climbed the stairs to the main floor. She found she had to cling on tightly to the wrought iron banister rail, as if she was slightly drunk and wobbly.

She first tried the kitchen, expecting to find April ready with her apologies. It was probably too late now to drive to a town to shop but if so, they could still go out for the evening. A chance to get out of the summery tops and shorts and into something dressier.

They could have a meal somewhere, she'd pay. After all, the villa stay had been free owing to April's friend and April had arranged everything else including all the food, so she felt it was her turn to return the kindness. Maybe, they could find a theatre or club in which to spend the rest of the evening, a pleasant change.

April wasn't in the lounge or out on the balcony. In fact, she wasn't anywhere in the villa and Sophie suddenly realised just how vast and empty the property was.

Could April have gone back to the beach to paint some more? Or even, finding Sophie sound asleep and not wishing to disturb her, was it possible she'd gone to find that village or town to stock up on essentials?

The garage, as with all the doors, was only opened with the keypad placed on the wall. It was shut tight, so Sophie couldn't tell if the car kept inside was missing. Her legs really didn't want to do her bidding, but she carefully made her way down the wooden steps to the beach.

Standing at the base she stared around, the beach was deserted, no sign of April or the boat which had been tethered to the small jetty.

Was that the answer to her friend's disappearance? She'd taken the boat with the outboard motor and sailed down the coast?

It was all very strange but then, she remonstrated with herself, April had every right to do and go where she wanted, she was on holiday too. It was surprising she hadn't left a note as she must have known, once Sophie woke from her nap, she'd wondered where she was.

A strengthening late afternoon breeze was blowing clouds in from the horizon and the water's edge rippled into waves.

Sophie shivered and wrapped her arms around her body. It was getting chilly and ominous clouds predicted a change in the weather sometime that night. Seagulls whirled and swooped overhead. She'd heard when the birds came on shore, it was a sure sign rain or a storm was on its way and for a few minutes contemplated if it was the truth, a myth or an old seaman's tale?

She was at a loss what to do next, but sensed her friend would return in time, and as for the trip, they could always do that another day. For now, she decided to go back indoors and make a cuppa, she was very thirsty all of a sudden.

More sea birds noisily swooped in, and amongst their raucous sound, Sophie thought she heard voices. They were distant, at first, and coming from the direction of the rock outcrop to her left. It was seconds later, she saw the two people, heads bent in deep conversation or argument, it was hard to tell at first.

She'd seen them before they both looked up and saw her. April Cox gave a semi-smile and half-heartedly raised a hand. The younger woman stopped and stared, but there was no welcoming smile on her features.

Chapter 5

He was not in the best frame of mind. In fact, as he marched into his office, he was fighting against the inner storm which threatened to erupt into a full-blown rage.

Jake Morgan's biggest strength was his ability to control his temper and right this moment he was struggling to stay calm and in control.

As a young entrepreneur back in the Thatcher era he'd began his successful businesses. He'd started buying and selling anything and everything from his bedroom in his parent's newly purchased council house. Over the proceeding years he'd built up an empire that included renovating and renting hundreds of properties, a string of betting and mobile phone shops, and only recently he'd added a payday money loaning enterprise. These were all very kosher and above board, but at times like this with the present uncertain climate he wasn't averse to making money by any other means.

Right now, Morgan was needing a speedy injunction of cash. It was in the middle of a recession, the banks were panicking and foreclosing on all loans and overdrafts, and this was a bad time to have a serious cash flow problem. Then his way out of his current monetary fix had come via a contact overseas and, after negotiating the deal, the shipment was due to land in the next few days.

Of course, Morgan, the honest, successful businessman was used to being wined and dined by the establishment he had a successful image to maintain. Why only the previous evening he'd been a guest at the Chamber of Commerce dinner, along with other VIP's pledging to keep the financial and commerce sector afloat in such bad times. He had to keep up the illusion of wealth and prosperity, or all the years of 'playing with the big boys' would come crashing down.

He was not prepared to let that happen. He enjoyed this lifestyle mixing with the rich and famous, properties here and abroad, his kids at private school and Gemma having designer clothes. He knew the value of her collection of Gucci handbags and Jimmy Choo shoes alone, could probably pay off most of his lesser debts but he had an image to keep up.

So, his plan to bring in the large consignment and sell on as quickly as he could, before the law got wind of it, could ultimately save his bacon.

It had been going so well. Everything was in place. Until he got wind of that particular bombshell and he'd had to rethink his plans and at such short notice.

Making sure he'd not be disturbed: right outside his office his PA was going through the daily post, and he knew he could leave most of it to her, or one of the other members of his staff, to reply either by phone or email. Anything not in his secretary's remit she would leave on his desk for later.

He sat at his desk, the day was going to be another hot one, but Morgan's only concession to the excess summer heat was to pull down his tie and undo the top button on his silk shirt. He'd already noted the expensive air conditioning was blasting out a chill enough to cool down the ice flow, and he'd already given instruction to his maintenance team to get it switched down to the lowest setting. His staff in the other offices, had plenty of water coolers and fountains to help keep their temperatures down, so he wasn't about to indulge them with the unnecessary over-use of conditioning, no matter how much they or the Union griped about working conditions. They hadn't to think about the costs of keeping this building and their jobs on track.

He unlocked the bottom drawer of his desk and pulled out the pay-as-u-go phone he'd picked up a couple of days ago from one of his mobile phone shops. He kept it locked away from prying eyes for just such a time, and speed dialled the only name and number in the log.

'Yes Boss.'

It was answered just as quickly, as if the man on the other end had been waiting for this moment.

'Now listen Lyall,' he had no time for niceties.

'Our 'bargaining tool' is in place so I think the man will have no option but to agree to my terms.'

Kyall Clark listened. He had no need to be enlightened, he'd already been told of the arrangements and now knew Jake's plan by heart. It might not have been the most original, but it was definitely the most daring, but then there was a lot at stake.

But then Jake had always played it close to the wind, known what to do in a sticky situation, that was probably why the lads referred to him as Teflon when they were having a pint and a laugh down at the Kicking Donkey.

He had known Jake Morgan from their school days, during which he had been the butt of Morgan's bullying. He later was to ingratiate himself in numerous ways after Jake first set up his bedroom enterprise selling legit items, but doing a thriving illegal business in counterfeit goods and cigarettes. Kyall had been the one taking the biggest risks, working as goffer and general dog's body, although in Clark's eyes he was Jake's number two man, reliant on his discretion and loyalty.

'What do you want me to do?'

'Keep everyone close until the night of the drop, I can see no reason why it'll not go as planned. Then it'll be up to you and your lads to unload the goods onto the container lorries and get them stored in the warehouse until they are to be collected and distributed ten days later. It stands to reason the place is to be fully patrolled, guards, dogs, the lot, until then.'

'And the police?'

'Forget them. I have the 'bargaining tool' in place and someone on hand making sure it stays that way.'

Even as Kyall listened he could sense something was worrying Morgan.

'What is it Boss?'

'Unfortunately, the one 'babysitting' is unreliable. I'm not sure she can do as she's told, so I need a trustworthy back up. Any suggestions?'

Kyall Clark's heart sank. This was all part of tactics and motives, the ducking and diving, the sudden changes. It was true everything had worked out as planned in the past on these numerous jobs even if on more than one occasion they had been 'flying by the seat of their pants', but this time. Kidnap and a hostage? He wondered about Jake's frame of mind. Was he finally losing it, after Lady Luck had been on his side on every iffy deal in the past?

He sighed and gave the answer he knew Jake was waiting for: 'Ok Boss, leave it with me?'

Chapter 6

Detective Chief Inspector Richard Oxford alongside some of his own men, who had been seconded to the Special Ops, was trying to concentrate on fully listening to the Senior Investigating Officer Jim Telford, the leader of the taskforce.

The combined teams sat around the briefing room listening to the update. This was an important breaking case, accumulating in weeks of surveillance and intel gathering from Interpol and other major police forces and it could ultimately bring the end to organised crime run by a man who had been untouchable for years, until now. It was to be a huge result if the team could pull it off, and it was Richard who would be heading one of the sub teams.

He was only one part of a team, but a team which worked together, and he also knew it would take just one member whose mind was not completely on the job for it all to go pear shaped. He must stay focussed.

It was hard when he was worried about Sophie and the fact, he'd been unable to get in touch with his wife for nearly a week. Sophie had promised to let him know how she was on a daily basis, especially after her illness and it had been remiss of him not to get fuller details, but knowing Sophie of old, she would have hated him to make too much of a fuss. Maybe later when, if he had time he'd text Helen in the States, she'd be sure to know the exact address of this holiday home and, potentially, have news.

He must concentrate. It might be the best chance they had to arrest the supposedly respectable businessman, someone who had been on the police radar for some time and, more importantly, to stop dangerous goods entering the country.

'Right,' Telford was saying. 'Operation Taurus' will be the name of this covert operation and the night in question is the sixth of August – er,' Telford corrected himself. 'I meant to say Tuesday the fourth of August.

We now know, based on information received that a cargo ship, the Zenia, registered in Panama but owned by a legit Greek shipping company, will be docking at the city's main docks around midnight.' He paused, glancing round the seated officers, to make sure everyone was paying attention.

'This is vitally important. The authorities, harbour and customs will be given the ships manifest stating the cargo is large containers containing motor parts and ready assembled vehicles imported from the Far East. It will seem to be in order and then, the containers will be loaded onto lorries and driven to a vast storage warehouse on the outskirts. There the illegal cargo will be unloaded and packed ready for later distribution.'

He looked around the room gauging the expression on their faces.

'Any questions?'

'What's the value of this haul, Guv?' It was a question from the back of the room and the tanned, thick-set, self-assured DI Elliot Vincent who would have done well as a weightlifting Olympian.

'We can only estimate it at around ten million Euros,' the senior investigating officer answered as if the amount was of little interest and there were the customary reactions and mutterings from the teams.

'So, the main man is playing for high stakes,' said Vincent, continuing with a grin. 'I wouldn't mind a piece of that.'

The detective's closest neighbour, DI Ollie Hanson agreed with a matey thumbs up.

Jim Telford waited for silence.

An officer at the front, who'd been frantically scribbling on a pad as if writing down every word, suddenly spoke up. 'Sir, do we have the address for the warehouse?'

Telford considered his answer before he spoke. He knew, full well, there was someone in this team who was on the 'person of interest's' payroll, but discretion was key!

'We're working on it,' he answered cautiously, noticing the keen Gavin Stevens jotted this down.

'In any case, that's a daft enough question.' The 'mouthpiece' Vincent spoke up again sounding impatient with this inquiry. He nudged the man next to him, as if needing another to go along with his argument.

'And, if it all goes to plan on the night,' he smirked around at the others in the room, confident he was monetarily centre stage.

Telford waited while a few smutty remarks filtered around the room and the laughs died down.

'So, on the night we will allow the goods to be brought ashore before impounding the ship and its cargo and arresting its captain and crew. Then we round up and arrest the gang and so, the address of the warehouse would turn out to be an irrelevant detail. Right?'

There were nods and murmurs all round confirming he made a logical comment.

The SIO nodded and immediately ignored the man who had interrupted him. When once more he had the room's full attention, he went on to explain how the operation would pan out and was only momentarily distracted when someone's mobile phone pinged a text message.

Chapter 7

'Hi there, Sophie.' It was April who raised her hand in greeting, as the two women strolled closer. 'You're awake then?'

Sophie stood still waiting for them to come to her, and not bothering to give the obvious reply.

She felt odd, out of sorts, what her dad jokingly called discombobulated but this odd word, meaning confused, seemed to fit her present mood. She must have slept heavy and now awake she was lethargic and feeling sluggish, and the last thing she wanted was a complete stranger appearing as if from nowhere.

Who was she? Where had she come from? There were no other properties that close, so not another holiday maker deciding to drop in for a chat, then?

The younger woman, long blonde hair clipped back in a ponytail, the tips dyed pink was wearing tight shorts and a crop-top in the same matching colour, took off her designer sunglasses as they approached Sophie, but her deep blue eyes remained sullen and unfriendly.

'This is Lexie,' April introduced her. 'She's my niece, my sister's girl.'

Lexie said a lazy, 'Hi', then as if she wasn't interested in Sophie, replaced her sunglasses on her perfectly shaped nose and moved to walk ahead of the other two, towards the steps.

'I invited her to stay with us at the villa for a few days,' explained April. 'She's had a hard time of it of late, so I thought the change would do her good.'

Sophie, walking alongside her friend, was finding it hard to keep up. Her head felt heavy, and the same dull pain lingered somewhere between her ears, she couldn't have said exactly where, but she would go and take another couple of her prescription painkillers before it became a full-blown headache.

April didn't bother to expand on Lexie's 'hard time'.

'You were sound asleep, so I didn't want to wake you,' April was explaining. She stopped short of mentioning the defunct trip and evening meal out. She lifted her head to watch her niece climb the steps. It appeared she had no intention of waiting for her aunt or Sophie as if she knew exactly where she was going. 'So, you've been here before?' Sophie thought, keeping her thoughts to herself.

'How did she get here?' she asked, aloud this time.

April appeared lost in thought as they climbed the steps.

'What dear?'

Sophie hated that false endearment, especially from someone who was attempting to sound just that little bit superior.

'I said,' she snapped and regretted it instantly. 'How did your niece get here? Did she come by that boat?'

'What boat would that be, dear?'

'When we were out painting earlier, there was a boat, white about the size of a rowboat with an outboard motor. It was moored to that small wooden jetty. You must have seen it.'

'I didn't see a boat. You must have been mistaken — imagined it,' there was a hint of callousness in her next words. 'You have remembered to take your meds, you know you were warned about these lapses, dear?'

April didn't wait for a reply, but sped up towards the open door of the villa. 'Lexie came by road,' she added over her shoulder. 'She's already parked her car in the garage.'

Sophie sighed. Of course, that was how the young woman got here and the garage was certainly large enough to house another vehicle. Right now, as always, the heavy automatic and keypad-locked up-and-over door was securely closed.

'Yes,' she muttered under breath, knowing April was too far ahead to hear, as she followed slowly. 'I've taken my meds, thank you. And there was a boat, so you are either very short sighted – or lying.'

Not for the first time Sophie felt uneasy and wanted to know more about the newcomer but when she followed April into the kitchen, the woman, having glanced inside, turned round at the hallway, and started towards the stairs. 'Lexie must have gone straight to her room. She is very upset about a lover's tiff, so I'll just go and check on her.'

Sophie poured herself a long, chilled glass of ice from the jug in the fridge and leant her back against the cool door.

She wished her mind was clearer, her nap had left her brain feeling fuzzy, but she was sure it wasn't so fuzzy that she'd forgotten or mistaken some facts.

She was still leant against the fridge when April returned a few minutes later.

'She'll be fine,' she added cheerily as if her niece's state of mind would be uppermost in Sophie's mind.

'She's just unpacking.' The subject changed rapidly. 'I thought we could have salad for our evening meal. We could have it along with the seared tuna steak.'

Sophie pushed herself away and turned to open the door. It was then she saw the well-stocked salad container.

'I thought we'd run out of fresh salad ingredients. That was one of the reasons we were taking a drive out this afternoon, so we could do a spot of shopping.'

'Yes– well. I looked in on you and you were so sound asleep I didn't like to wake you. I was about to go alone, when Lexie arrived and thankfully, she'd had the foresight to shop on her way here.' She smiled across the room. 'Panic over, dear.'

It was on her tongue to snap, 'I wasn't panicking,' but Sophie held her words back. It wasn't like her to be confrontational, but she wished April didn't keep adding 'dear' as if she was having to explain to someone losing her mind. In Fact, it felt an odd kind of day, right from the start, as if April was beginning to regret coming on holiday with someone who was recuperating from a serious illness and realising the responsibility she'd taken on. Then the unexpected arrival of her troubled niece was only adding to the mix.

But it didn't add up.

'I thought you were all alone in the world, April. What's your sister's name?'

April glanced up from the work surface on which she'd been preparing the ingredients.

'I don't have a sister,' she said sharply.

'But I thought you said Lexie is your niece. You definitely introduced her as your sister's girl.'

'You're mistaken. I said Lexie is the daughter of my cousin.'

For a millisecond a look of concern passed over the other woman's face then she smiled as if understanding the other's dilemma. 'Oh my dear,' April said condescendingly. 'You are getting confused and I'm beginning to get concerned about you Sophie. Have you had another one of your headaches?'

Sophie blinked hard but didn't reply. Doubt and uncertainty filled her mind, maybe she had misunderstood or misheard.

There was an edge to the atmosphere in the large kitchen diner and it was silent, with only the screeching from the gulls outside the large plate glass window, until April said. 'Pour the wine, would you Sophie?' Her manner was again cordial and Sophie was wondering if she'd imagined the previous chill, but then today she was finding it hard to tell the difference.

April indicated the bottle of white left on the table alongside three wine glasses.

'I brought it up from the cellar – when you were asleep –.' There was that edge again, as if for some reason she resented or regretted her choice of holiday companion.

Sophie did her bidding, puzzled, and confused and noting it was a very fine and expensive bottle of French Chablis and wondering if their absent and invisible host would appreciate them dipping into his obvious extensive wine cellar?

'By the way, April,' Sophie thought it wiser to get back onto a neutral footing. 'Have you seen my mobile phone and charger? I thought I had both this morning in my canvas bag, but I can't remember if I left them somewhere.'

April put down the knife and started to arrange the salad into the serving bowl before answering. 'I've not seen them,' she said, her concentration on the food. 'I'm sure they'll turn up, but you have been forgetting things lately.'

Before Sophie could say anything, she continued. 'But like I told you, there's no signal out here, so a phone's no good to you.'

Sophie was about to refute that, but Lexie had wandered into the room and, ignoring the two, helped herself to one of the glasses and sat down at the breakfast bar. There she drank half before stating. 'I'm starving *Auntie*. What time will the food be ready?'

April laughed out loud, but not before Sophie had seen her angry expression. It was a coarse, forced laugh.

'I was just telling Sophie how your mum and I are cousins. 'Course that hasn't stopped Lexie from calling me Auntie April. Has it?' Sophie thought she was over emphasising the relationship as if it mattered but let it go.

The younger woman fiddled with her hair and shrugged as if it was immaterial, then helped herself to another full glass.

The food was perfect, but then Sophie readily conceded April was an excellent cook whereas she could hardly cook anything that wasn't already prepared, frozen and destined for the microwave.

Hardly anyone spoke during the meal and even before the cheese platter had been placed on the table, Lexie helped herself to the last of the wine, slid open the glass doors and settled on a sunbed on the balcony listening to loud music coming from her ear buds she'd routed out from an extra-large beach bag. It was just half past nine and the sun, making its way earthwards to the horizon, sent light bouncing off the ocean to form patterns on the sheer glass.

April's eyes followed her relative outside and it seemed she could read Sophie's thoughts.

'You must excuse Lexie,' she unconsciously folded her paper napkin into two then four. 'She's not usually so unsociable, but she's very unhappy with her fella. I was hoping for a break away would help her get over him.'

'It doesn't matter,' said Sophie. 'I suppose we've all been there.'

She hoped it sounded more sincere than she felt, she was desperate to contact Richard. Just a familiar voice and a few hours away from this villa, which was beginning to feel more claustrophobic and alien, would have been a welcomed distraction.

Her companion didn't comment so Sophie decided to change the subject hoping that by the morning, Lexie would be in a better frame of mind. As it was, what had started as a pleasant break with a like-minded artist friend, in just a few hours had taken on a strange atmosphere.

'I'll help you load the dishwasher but then I think I'll turn in.' Sophie yawned. 'I'm suddenly feeling tired.'

April smiled and nodded. 'You need as much rest as you can get, after what you've been through. Leave the dishes, I can do them. Perhaps in the morning, if you're feeling up to it, we could take that drive into town and do some shopping?'

'I'd like that,' Sophie agreed, her mood changing to one of anticipation. 'See you in the morning.' She yawned deeply again and discounted going to the young woman on the balcony, instead she said to April. 'Goodnight!'

Chapter 8

'Sir, I think you need to see these.'

When the teams had finished being briefed on Operation Taurus, Detective Chief Inspector Oxford had held back to be the last left in the room alongside SIO Jim Telford.

'The videos were sent to my phone a few minutes ago, but I thought it wiser to wait until the others had gone.'

Telford, the senior officer in charge, repositioned his glasses, kept on top of his head to the tip of his fleshy nose. The man at his side was a good six inches taller, probably two stone lighter and he'd known Richard Oxford for over twenty years when, even as a wet-behind-the-ears rookie he'd considered him sensible, level-headed, and definitely not prone to over-reacting, but now Oxford looked worried, not only worried but scared. His usual tanned skin was grey, and he appeared in a state of shock.

'To be frank I don't know what to do,' he confessed. 'I thought Sophie was on holiday with a friend,' he told Telford. 'I suppose I should have shown more interest when she talked about this new friend April or Avril, she'd met through art classes. A hobby was just what she needed, and when she told me they'd booked a holiday cottage for a fortnight to do more painting, I was pleased she was having a break after what she'd been through. I'm ashamed to say I had other things on my mind, like the upcoming Operation Taurus. I have no idea who this woman is.'

He stopped the tirade and pointed to the phone's screen.

'Look at these. They've been taken on my wife's phone and sent to mine,' he paused.

'They are images of Sophie — my wife.' His mouth was dry, his tongue sticking to the roof of his mouth, and he seemed unable to coordinate his thoughts.

He waited, unable to move or speak, while Telford looked at the screen. He slowly flicked to the three clear images. It was the same woman lying fully clothed on the top of a bed, apparently asleep, in a very white room. It could have been any room in any holiday home, or even a boutique hotel, except it didn't look to be of the usual general standard.

'At first I thought she was dead,' Richard said, the tone giving away his true feelings of dread.

The SIO didn't speak but watched the images closely, listening to the sound-over, obviously made using a voice distorter so it was impossible to tell the gender of the person.

'We have Sophie Oxford, wife of DCI Richard Oxford and she will be held as a hostage until you cancel your planned raid on the cargo ship, the Zenia, when she docks next month. If you still go ahead and ignore this warning, then the woman will pay with her life.'

That dramatic statement accompanied the first of the video images. The wording of each could have been put together either by someone of average intelligence, or more likely someone pretending to be.

'If you think you can still stop our operation to bring the shipment ashore, then

know this, SIO Telford, we will know if your plan stays the same.'

There was no voice recording alongside the last image. It was still Sophie, on the bed in the same position, her eyes closed and there was no sign of life.

Richard interrupted Telford's thoughts. 'I should have got more of the details, but when Sophie assured me, she'd be keeping in touch with text and phone calls, I left it at that. I was beginning to worry, it's almost a week since she last phoned to tell me she was fine and enjoying the peace and quiet, but didn't really say much about the actual place except it was a private and remote from any other civilization.' The words ran away from him, and he sounded confused and only just in control.

'Do you think this was all planned and this artist woman was involved in this — this kidnap?' Richard rubbed his forehead with frustration and pointed at the mobile phone's screen and didn't wait for Telford's comments.

Richard repeated,' I thought she was dead.' Her husband cleared his throat. 'She has been so sick, and I nearly lost her then, so–.'

Jim Telford replayed the video segments.

'But then you saw that slight movement of her hand in scene two? As I did. Sophie is asleep in those pictures.'

'Probably drugged?'

The senior officer nodded but didn't say: 'They must have had this planned for a few weeks, so I'm guessing they're panicked with so much at stake.'

Instead, he added. 'But importantly she's still alive. You said you received these how long ago?'

Richard indicated the date and time on his phone.

'So, about twenty minutes ago. We can assume, whoever it is that is holding her, can't risk harming her as long as they see her as a bargaining tool.'

He wanted to reassure the man standing beside him. If Oxford fell apart now, then it would be understandable if he turned 'rogue' and took it upon himself to act irrationally and alone.

'I can imagine if my wife was in danger and of course I'd move heaven and earth to get her back safely, but for now we mustn't react, that's what they'll be expecting. We must keep this strictly between ourselves. Just you and me.'

He was thoughtful, working out in his own mind how best to play this.

'Now look, this is what I think would be the best way to go from here. You and I must do everything we can to find out where Sophie is being held and get her out, but in the meantime and assuming we are not successful, her safety is paramount. So, we do as instructed and as there are only five days before the Zenia is officially due to dock, we must play the balancing act. So this is what we do, tell the Operation Taurus team I've had a tip off that the date has been altered – I don't know, bad weather has put back the date for docking or something. I now tell the team the due date will be the night of the sixth and so the planned raid is now for that night.'

Oxford looked puzzled as if he was having trouble keeping up.

Jim Telford took a deep breath before saying more. It was just as likely Oxford would go and confront the head of this criminal gang and everything, the police raid, confiscation of the illegal cargo, possibly the safety of Sophie Oxford and it could all go horribly wrong.

'Richard, we have no other option. Your wife could be killed if Morgan thinks we double crossed him. We have to be really careful; I know someone on the team is on Morgan's payroll so we must look as if we came up with a viable option and sent Special Ops on a wild goose chase.'

'A double bluff?' asked the anxious man.

'A double bluff,' answered his superior. 'You know you are too close to this, and I should be taking you off the case.'

Telford didn't pause knowing Oxford would fiercely object.

'We must play it this way although it could all go tits up but at least take a step back and look into who this April woman is? What does the art class know about her? They're bound to have contact details, her address etc? Is she involved, or is it just a coincidence? Although I doubt that's the case.'

He would be playing a dangerous game and the hostage could still be harmed, but he knew he had little or no other options.

'Ok?' he stared at the man seated opposite.

'Ok,' Oxford answered.

Chapter 9

She thought she'd been woken from a deep sleep by the sound of a car, but she could have dreamt it.

The sun was already high in the sky and when she checked the time on her small travel clock, she kept on her bedside table, it read half past eleven. She had slept for hours, a troubled sleep packed with strange dreams bordering on nightmares.

Never mind. A new day and they were going out for a drive, a chance to see other people and places. Sophie climbed out of bed, had a quick shower, and dressed in peppermint green casual loose-fitting trousers, matching top and flat sandals. Her choice of outfit was cool enough to saunter around shops, but neat enough to go to an upmarket restaurant for dinner, if the day warranted it.

She was looking forward to a change.

On her way up the stairs to the main floor she glanced at the three other doors leading to the other two bedrooms and the wine cellar. They were all closed, with the one door having the customary six-digit keypad. So it was likely, at this time of day, she was the last up. At the back of her mind, she was miffed that April, having promised the day out shopping and sightseeing, had let her lie in, but then again April was thinking of her recent illness and perhaps didn't want to disturb her if she was sleeping so soundly. After a week she was certainly doing that, it had to be the calming tranquillity of the place plus the fresh sea air.

The huge kitchen diner was empty, but she could see Lexie stretched out on a sunbed beyond the balcony doors. The younger woman was now wearing a beachwear outfit of bra top and sarong, in shades of mauve and turquoise, which highlighted her sunbed tanned limbs and made the tattoos across her shoulders and neck stand out against the intense shade of 'orangey-brown'. A collection of gold slave bangles jangled around both wrists and she'd even had time, in the last few hours to add purple streaks to her long hair to compliment her outfit.

Lexie didn't look up from painting her toenails which matched her long Shellac nails, as Sophie pushed open the door and stepped outside.

'Morning.' Lexie didn't acknowledge the greeting but concentrated on the nail, wriggling her toes as she went on to the next.

'Where's April?' Sophie asked. 'We were supposed to be going for a drive.'

'Oh she left early,' she fished in the large bag at her side then wedged a shaped piece of foam between her finished toes and started on the next nail.

Sophie sat on the neighbouring sunbed. She was surprised just how disappointed she was feeling.

'I thought I imagined hearing a car,' she said, her gaze going beyond the coast and towards the rolling waves far out to sea.

'She went about nine. She said she had chores but I'm guessing she was going to look for a bookie in the nearest town.' That was the most Lexie had said to Sophie since she'd arrived.

'A bookie?'

'Mmm. A bookmaker. Someone who takes bets on horses and things,' Lexie said as if explaining to a child.

'Yes I know what a bookie is, but why couldn't she have waited for me? She could have gone to place a bet, while I went into Boots to buy sun cream and a hair conditioner?'

Sophie was getting used to her hair's cropped length but since its regrowth, following her operation and now peppered with streaks of silver, it seemed fine and dull.

'Dunno,' was the reply she got.

'By the way,' Sophie asked intrigued. 'Is April your aunt or cousin?'

'We're not related,' Lexie answered, concentrating on the other foot, then adding, as if by way of this explanation meant 'end of questions'.

'Her mum knows my mum; you know how it is? I've always called her aunty.'

Sophie didn't know whether this was true, she seemed to be getting conflicting answers to everything.

'OK and she went early to place a bet?'

'Mm. 'Aunty April' has a problem. A gambling problem,' her plumped out lips had difficulty forming a successful sneer, so it made her face appear to grimace. 'She puts money on anything horses, dogs but her real 'pash' is rolling the dice and card games, especially craps. So, if she finds a private game or a casino, she might be gone for days or until she loses even more money, because she loses more than she ever wins. Nothing stops dear Aunty April.'

Sophie was amazed. She would never have dreamt that her 'friend' had such a secret, but then again, how much did she really know about April Cox?

'Has she not tried to get help?'

Lexie rolled her eyes. 'You mean Gamblers Anonymous? Oh yeah, but it hasn't helped someone like her, though. She can't stop and now she's up to her eyes in debt with some very iffy people.'

She stood suddenly and snatched at her bottle of nail polish and the other paraphernalia on the small wicker table at her side, and with an unwarranted glare at Sophie marched back inside.

'I'm going to take a long, hot bath,' she snapped, and Sophie had a feeling she'd regretted revealing so much about the absent woman.

Chapter 10

Richard Oxford knocked on the SIO's office door.

'Come in.' Through the glass panel he could see the team of Special Ops, heads bent over their computer monitors going over the new details of the raid. Almost all accepted the change of date and location, and Telford was sure the newly planned 'fake' raid was what Jake Morgan was waiting to hear. Nevertheless, as he waited for DCI Oxford to close the door, he was aware of just how much the hostage's husband was holding up. It had to be a terrible strain, not knowing what was happening to Sophie and still keeping professional.

Richard spoke first.

Apart from a couple of exceptions everyone's onboard, and it wouldn't feel right if Vincent, and his oppo DI Ollie Hanson, didn't back him up with a moan or complain about just about everything. As expected, the ever keen and scrupulous DI Steven's has written and logged every new move. That officer's a real stickler for dotting the 'i's' and crossing the 't's'.' Richard said, perching on the corner of the desk.

'What did Hanson and Vincent have to say?'

'Oh, the usual. Ollie and his wife had plans for the sixth, a meal out with the in-laws and he's 'taking stick' from the missus on that score. While the big fella wanted to watch some sporting programme on the telly, so I told him he could always watch it on Freeview, but it was still a chance for Vincent to have a good moan.'

Telford nodded and sat back in his swivel desk chair. He didn't comment. Almost all the people on the other side of the closed door were top class coppers.

'Just to let you know, I received a text on my phone earlier.' He showed the image to Richard. 'I could hardly keep this to myself. From the date and time recorder it was sent to my phone twenty minutes ago and once again it was from Sophie's phone. It must have been switched off as soon as it was sent, because there's no way to track the signal back.'

It was a video of Sophie walking alone along a beach. To her left was the sea that could have indicated in the far distance a curve in the landscape like a bay, but it was hard to tell and could have been one of thousands of bays or inlets on the numerous islands and coasts, around the entire UK coastline.

Presumably the same distorted voice-overstated, without any sign of emotion:

'Sophie Oxford is still alive and well and she will stay that way, as long as Project Taurus keeps to the agreement.'

Richard swore.

'If that monster hurts her —.'

The SIO sympathised.

'I know Richard, but we must keep our heads. We are following the man's orders to the letter, once he knows for sure he might let her go.'

'Or he'll keep her his prisoner until he's got away with the valuable goods, he's not likely to risk losing them. If we could just locate that beach and coastline, we might be able to rescue Sophie and then arrest Morgan and his 'merry men'.' The chief inspector ground his teeth with frustration and fear.

He sighed and Telford waited for him to continue.

'I've been trying to find out what I can about this woman on holiday with my wife,' Richard said. 'We are assuming she is part of the hostage conspiracy.'

'And what have you found out?'

'Not much. April Cox registered with the college mid-course, around a fortnight after my wife started the same watercolour lessons. About the same time, we got the tip off about this huge consignment on its way to British waters, so it's more than a coincidence. I believe she was told to get to know Sophie just in case things didn't quite pan out. There's just too much at stake and Cox taking Sophie to God- knows-where was a back-up plan.'

Telford listened closely but didn't comment.

'Cox attended the two lessons a week until the summer term came to an end, and the art tutor confirmed that April and my wife seemed to bond and quickly become friends. He was complimentary about both students telling me Sophie's work was good and showed promise, if she kept it up and intended to return in September. As for April Cox she was turning out to have a latent talent and he hoped to have the chance to encourage her gift.

He also confirmed he hadn't seen or heard from his star pupil since, but that was not surprising as he'd flown out to join an arty commune on Mykonos the following day, and only returned yesterday.'

Oxford was struggling to keep this professional, all the time his mind on his absent wife. Clearing his throat, he added the rest of his research.

'The college records have only basic contact details, her address, email and phone numbers. Not surprising she is unknown at the block of flats she gave as her address and the email and phone numbers don't exist. So, who is April Cox?'

Chapter 11

Sophie had lost interest in her painting and the reason she'd come on this break with April.

The rest of the hours stretched out to an inevitable sunset, and as she strolled along the empty shore with only the sea, the small jetty, the top half of the villa visible from her viewpoint, she was overcome by homesickness.

This grew worse with the only other person, the increasingly hostile Lexie now spending most of the days on the balcony. What of the absent April, wherever she was?

'Do you think April will be back today,' she'd asked Lexie mid-afternoon.

'Dunno,' the younger woman didn't bother to look up.

'Well, I want to go, but I'll need to explain my decision to April.'

'Go? Where?'

'Home.'

Lexie removed her sunglasses and stared at Sophie.

'Why?' she asked, as if such a quest was unbelievable.

'Because I want to. This break hasn't worked out as I thought it would — and I miss my family.'

Lexie shrugged her bare shoulders and replaced her glasses, before settling back against the sunbed's pillow.

'Whatever!'

Sophie was left feeling disconcerted by the woman's complete disinterest. She wanted to leave. She wanted to go home to a familiar place to be back with Richard, although he would be at work for hours if not days until she saw him again, he was always on the end of a phone. As were her parents, her sister Helen and Kirstie.

Her precious Kirstie, ten, moody, argumentative, yet all these feelings of confusion, hurt and fear were understandable. She was too young to have to cope with more worries on her young shoulders than anyone of her age should have to carry. Her daughter had not understood her mother's illness, the hours on an operating table and then the slow recovery back to a parent that seemed to have changed in so many ways.

Sophie missed her daughter more than she could ever have imagined and not being able to phone, text, email or see her, or any member of her family, was a very lonely feeling.

Late afternoon and with no sign of April Sophie wandered aimlessly along the beach close to the water's edge, stumbling slightly as the toe of her flip flop caught against a sparse ridge of sand. She stopped and hesitated, something had caught the peripheral of her vision and peered back towards the villa. Had she seen a momentary flash of light, like the dipping sun on a mirror or glass or even a camera lens, coming from the villa's direction, or was it her imagination? She cupped her hands around her eyes to block out the surrounding light and to see better, but whatever it was, if it had been real, was gone as quickly.

Sophie turned again to resume her stroll along the beach, and her unease and uncertainty intensified.

She could hardly wait until the morning when she hoped April would have returned. If she wanted to stay with her 'niece' and have the remaining week without the third, it would possibly suit Lexie who had been hostile towards her from the first. She'd ask April to drive her to the nearest town or railway station and the more she thought about it, the better she was beginning to feel. Her head still felt heavy, and she was slightly disoriented, but she'd made a decision, and her optimism had grown after a restless night. The next morning, somewhat relieved that for once she didn't feel as if she'd slept heavily or that her head was full of cotton wool she quickly showered and dressed.

It had been frustrating when, having waited up for April to return, she'd eventually given in to weariness around one a.m. and probably missed her return, but now she could start to pack her case and get ready to leave.

It was still only seven when Sophie found the other two-bedroom doors were closed and the cellar door locked. She climbed the stairs to the main floor suddenly feeling optimistic and confident she'd find her new friend, as she had on many of the other mornings, in the kitchen or on the balcony. She might even find April had taken up her usual position on the beach and was working on another watercolour composition.

She didn't find April, and, from the height of the balcony, she could look down to the beach, to the jetty, and there was no sign of life apart from a few circling gulls high in the pale blue sky.

The place on this level was empty and had a strange echoing sound, giving the place an air of being abandoned. Starting with the bedroom Sophie went from room to room calling the women's names and growing more and more puzzled and concerned.

Although she guessed the solid garage door would be down, so no way to tell if one or both cars were still inside, she would still go and look and see if April and Lexie were on the beach. It seemed the most sensible action, but she couldn't ignore her growing panic, or the sense something was very wrong.

The beautifully figured marble not only covered the floors in all the main rooms, but the large double height hallway. Sophie crossed the expanse to the only outer door and there fully expected to keycode to release the powerful locks. It was the same memorable pin number used by them, since their arrival and just another one of the many security features in the villa.

She typed in the number, but the red light on the pad continued to stare like an angry bloodshot eye confirming its authority. The light should have turned green and then she would have been able to hear the faint sound of the locking mechanism effortlessly working, releasing the massive, solid door. The door stayed firmly locked.

Had she put in the wrong sequence or mistyped? She tried it for the second time and the red light steadfastly remained.

For the third time, she tried it again but this time slowly pinning in the six digits she knew was the correct pin number.

Nothing happened.

'Oh, for crying out loud,' Sophie exploded, adding a selection of choice words aimed at the stubborn lock and door.

Slowly the truth dawned and the realisation the pin number, to open the main door, had been altered and Sophie caught her breath with surprise but mainly with a sudden overwhelming dread.

Why? Why would either April or Lexie, or both women change the code without telling her the new numbers? There had to be a plausible answer and maybe she could put this latest confusion down to her still muddled brain, but even as she turned away from the door and walked back to the living area, it didn't make sense.

Where were April and Lexie? Had they deliberately left, she had no way of knowing if their cars were still in the garage. The truth was that alone in this luxury villa somewhere along the coast, – a coast, she didn't recognise, with no communication or a way to get outside help, she was virtually stranded.

Chapter 12

'What is going on?' Sophie asked the empty, sparsely, if tastefully furnished holiday villa as if the smooth plastered walls would give her an answer.

She pushed open the panels leading from the living area to the outside, grateful that at least those doors had basic locking bolts top and bottom and meant she could take gulps of fresh sea air. Stepping onto the expanse of the balcony floor, she glanced at the arrangement of seating and small side tables. Hardly coming as a surprise to find that, apart from a couple of discarded tissues and a bottle of sun cream, they were vacant of the bare-limbed Lexie.

She crossed to the waist high glass barrier that surrounded the balcony, and looked down at the beach below. There was no safe way down, even if she attempted the climb over the barrier and the outcrop that made up the foundation of the villa, it had to be a good six metres drop to the scattered rocks below.

And if she did, where would she go, to get away from this place that was fast becoming a prison?

The sea, the beach, even the old wooden jetty were permanent, except the small boat had gone — even supposing she'd not imagined it in the first place. She was beginning to doubt anything was real.

Sophie gripped the edge of the rail until her white knuckles stood out against her tanned hands. Far out to sea the darkening sky of a distant storm was turning the horizon a deep, angry purple.

None of this made sense. Where were April and Lexie? What had happened overnight that they should leave her alone and stranded?

Bemused, Sophie slowly shook her head, even the swirling wings and the sharp cries of the seagull appeared to have deserted her this morning. 'I don't understand. What is happening?'

The suddenness of a voice, in the strange quietness of the place, made her jump so violently she thought her heart would stop.

'I thought you'd have worked it out by now.'

Sophie spun round to find Lexie standing just behind her. The same belligerent young woman who had gone out of her way to be distant and sullen at best, and uncommunicative, almost rude, at worst.

'Oh it's you,' Sophie said, recovering quickly. 'Where have you come from? I've already looked in all the rooms — and why have you changed the code on the front door keypad?'

Lexie swung her bag on her shoulder and perched on the nearest sunbed, nonchalantly examined her fingernails before speaking.

'You can't have looked properly.' She stretched, as if she'd only recently woken.

'Where's your aunt or cousin, or whatever April is to you?' Sophie asked, conscious that she wasn't getting any relevant answers from the woman.

'We're not related, I thought you'd got that,' she added, her gaze going beyond Sophie as she concentrated on the line of purple out at sea. 'Looks like we're in for a storm later.'

She once again studied her immaculate nails before giving an answer.

'April's gone.'

'Gone where? When? Why hasn't she let me know her plans?'

Lexie shrugged unconcerned.

'Don't know. What she does has nothing to do with me. All I know is she came back last night, after you'd gone to bed and then took off before dawn.' She grinned, but it was without humour. 'I think she'd lost a 'packet' on the gaming tables and now there's even more people after her,' her explanation was tinged with more malice. 'I told you she's a serious gambler, didn't I?'

Sophie had had enough. She was being manipulated and she wanted answers. She marched resolutely across the balcony to the sunbed, beside Lexie's, and sat on the edge facing her.

'Right,' she meant business. 'For some reason I was brought here to this isolated luxury and now I'm unable to leave. In fact, I'm being held here against my will. I don't believe you when you said April left, I've looked in her room and her things are still here. I wouldn't be surprised if her car is still in the garage. So you are going to tell me exactly what this is all about.'

The change in Lexie was so sudden that Sophie was taken aback. Previously Lexie had been unfriendly and offhand now she was angry and offensive. She turned to face Sophie, her expression sneering and unpleasant.

'I didn't want to come here, but my boyfriend told me to. I was to keep tabs on you and 'Aunty' April and make sure she kept to the deal, and you behaved yourself. Believe me I've hated every minute, but I had no option.'

'I don't understand.'

Lexie exploded, 'Of course you don't understand. Let me tell you, you weren't meant to understand. Just to stay here and stay out of the way.'

She visibly relaxed and leant back against the overstuffed cushion, closing her eyes.

'I'll tell you. Why not? It's not as if you can tell anyone. It's about millions. More money than I could ever dream of, and me and Lyall's cut. The Boss has this fantastic scheme: there's a container ship with an expensive and illegal cargo, and it's due to dock on the fourth. The goods are set to make us all very rich.'

She was already spending her share in her mind and her face softened.

'Then just as everything is in place, the Boss learns that the police know all about it and are planning a clandestine raid on the night and guess who will be leading this raid?'

She didn't wait for a reply.

'A certain senior office by the name of DCI Richard Oxford,' the expression on Lexie's face changed again to one of spite and resentment, as if it had been a personal slight aimed solely at her and her boyfriend.

Sophie waited, wanting to know everything.

'He's a clever man, is the Boss and he wasn't about to give up on the best deal of a lifetime, so he came up with this hostage plan. Originally it was to be Oxford's wife and kid, but daughter went abroad so it left you. The deal was Oxford, and his team of 'Action Men', was to play dumb, pretend they'd got the wrong night so the goods would be offloaded and disposed of to a ready buyer, and you'd get to live.

She continued without emotion or empathy.

'It was up to 'dear old aunty' April to do her part. She already owes a lot of dangerous people, money lenders and bookies, a lot of money and she was given a way of getting all her debts paid by becoming your new best friend and offering you a free holiday.'

'So who does this villa belong to?'

'The Boss of course. He owns lots of property here and overseas and he has oodles of power and wealth, but as he says, 'you can't have too much money, can you?'

It was a lot to take in yet even as she listened to this unreal scenario, certain anomalies, during her days here, were becoming clearer. Not least that she had been drugged, probably with sleeping pills on a nightly basis, and that would account for her continued feeling of listlessness.

Until this morning and now she was beginning to think straight. Presumably there hadn't been a chance to spike her food or drink the previous night, because up to then how else would they have stopped her from questioning some of the strange goings on?

'Who is he? This mystery 'Boss'?' He must be quite something if he thinks he can pull off some huge crime and kidnap a policeman's wife, and get away with it.'

'Jake Morgan,' Lexie looked to be impressed with the man.

'Never heard of him,' Sophie said, her words edged with derision.

Lexie ignored her and just a small smile lifted the corners of her mouth, revealing her delight and contempt at Sophie's dilemma.

'So, What happens now? Now I know what you, and the leader of the gang, is up to? I mean you can't keep me here for much longer. What happens when, and if, Morgan is successful, and the police hold back letting him get away with the cargo? Do you just let me go?'

Sophie almost didn't add the last sentence to her question, fearful of the answer.

'The original plan was to leave you here, when we were clear and out of the country.'

'And?'

'And I now think you are becoming an unnecessary liability,' she grinned as if she had suddenly understood a private joke. 'April was telling me about your illness and the operations. She said your heart actually stopped twice and you had to be resuscitated.' She laughed out loud at the thought. 'Just like in that film Flatliners. What a blast!'

She paused her narrative, her attention taken by the first clap of thunder and a flash of lightning far out at sea.

Sophie took a deep breath and in that second, she knew her proposed fate.

'Your boss has no intention of letting me go. He probably had that in mind from the beginning.'

Lexie didn't deny it.

'He intends to kill me for a third time and this time there'll be no machine to save me.'

Chapter 13

Now the truth was out in the open Lexie went back to ignoring her, only her previous sullenness and uncommunicative mood remained, while Sophie sat staring at the incoming storm trying to work things out in her mind. The sky immediately overhead had quickly turned to an angry grey tinged with a sulphurous yellow.

She hardly noticed the change in the weather as she was still trying to process this revelation. It was unbelievable that it had been an elaborate plan with her used as bait, as a hostage, to make sure her husband and the team turned a blind eye to a crime in two days' time. Did this really happen in the twenty-first century? It all seemed very much a 'boys own adventure story'. And she still didn't know what the cargo was to be, assuming cocaine or other drugs being the most obvious. They wouldn't go to such elaborate details and planning for anything less.

It was quite a dilemma.

On the one hand the illegal goods, whatever they were, would be allowed into the country unhindered by the authorities. Or NCA and customs called Morgan's bluff, ignored the threats against her and actually went ahead with the planned raid? Either way she could end up being the scapegoat. She could lose her life!

No that wasn't right! Richard wouldn't let anything happen to her. He'd been right at her side throughout her prognosis and operation and treatment. He loved her, although they had their problems.

But what could he, or the Special Ops team, be able to do assuming they knew this would not end well?

Sophie pondered this. Trying to think of a way out of this dire situation. Essentially, she was locked in property with top-of-the range security, so a prisoner and, as far as she could tell, miles away from civilization.

She didn't realise she'd spoken aloud, until Lexie turned her head to stare at her.

'Yes, there was a boat. My boyfriend brought me here in his speed boat and stayed overnight. It was a wee bit annoying when you said you'd seen it, but April came up with your failing memory or imagination as an excuse. If you were hoping for a boat or some other way to get away. Then forget it.'

As if she'd not spoken, she turned away and closed her eyes once more.

So Lexie hadn't come by car after all.

But this woman had to have some way of communication with the outside world. The more she thought about it, the more it was making sense. This villa, with its top-of-the-range decor, furniture, even security, of course there had to be a Wi-Fi and telephone system. The question is, where? And what has happened to April?

'Where are you going?'

It wasn't a police enquiry, more of a charged question made to a prisoner by her gaoler. Lexie opened one eye as Sophie got to her feet, making for the ceiling-height glass doors and back inside.

'I have a headache coming on, probably because of the impending storm. I'm going to rest on my bed.'

She was fed up with this woman's attitude and, now she knew Lexie's real reason for being here, she saw no reason to hide her resentment.

'Anything wrong with that? Or do I have to ask your permission if I want to pee?'

The woman, with the accompanying bag dropped on the floor and completely relaxed on the sunbed, shrugged. In Lexie's mind this would all be over in a couple of days when the goods were in the country, they'd be rich and Kyall would be coming for her in his boat. She'd have no need to nursemaid this policeman's wife any longer and basically, she didn't really care what Sophie did from now on. What happened to her afterwards was not Lexie's problem.

She waved a dismissive hand. 'Whatever,' and closed her eyes again, in fact she was growing bored with this whole situation.

She was already imagining being with Kyall on a white sandy, Caribbean beach, palm trees, a smooth, calm deep blue ocean and they were sipping cocktails. This fantasy was far removed from the irritation of DCI Oxford's wife, and as for April she was already no more than a disposable irritation. There were too many exciting plans for the future to dwell on the past.

Sophie stayed calm and first tried the number sequence to open the heavy main door. She was momentarily surprised it didn't open. So the others had already changed the key code and she was locked inside. She made for the staircase down to the bedrooms, not surprisingly Lexie's was locked, she half expected that. Sophie next tried April's door and turned the handle expecting the same, but it opened easily, and she stepped inside. Just like the other rooms, the decor was predominately white the furnishing sparse but luxurious.

Sophie took a quick look round. It was filled with April's painting paraphernalia, bare and finished canvases rested against the cupboard, while the pallet, a collection of brushes and a box of watercolour paints were on the top. They were the only items laid out in a tidy formation, because the room was cluttered with clothing flung across the bed and a chair and an accumulation of toiletries and makeup containers littered every available surface. It was almost as if it had been randomly searched.

Lexie?

In the wardrobe in a more ordered fashion were clothes on hangers and shoes and sandals stacked on rack Her suitcases were pushed to the back.

So, whatever had happened to April? Her 'friend' had left without taking her stuff with her. Was it possible her car was still in the garage?

Of course, she herself was virtually locked inside the villa and without knowing the codes to open any of the locks. She was momentarily amused at the idea that someone would go to the trouble, and at great expense, to turn a luxury villa into a fortress.

She paused, giving herself precious time to think it through. She was in great danger, there was no getting round that, and she had to escape. Supposing she could get the lock combination and get past Lexie without being seen? Was

April's car conveniently in the garage, useful if she could work out the code to that key lock? But what good would that be if she didn't have April's car keys? It was one puzzle after another, a veritable maze of confusion.

Sophie sat on the bed amongst the clutter and rested her head in her hands. She really was starting with a headache, the last thing she needed if she was to get out of this frightening situation.

The drawer in the bedside cupboard was closed, so maybe it had been missed in an early search. Something told Sophie the earlier search by Lexie had been done in a frenzy of pique and not necessarily a systematic logical search. She leant across and pulled open the drawer. It didn't take long to find hidden beneath a packet of tissues, a bottle of sleeping pills. These had more than likely been the ones in her food or drink each evening. She placed the bottle in the side pocket of her jeans and began going through the other untouched drawers in the room. It didn't take long to find some very interesting objects.

Sophie located April's car keys on a fob in her handbag pushed into one of the cupboards and they joined the bottle in her pants pocket. There was no sign of her phone, charger or what would have been April's mobile.

She paused; sure she had heard something overhead. Perhaps Lexie was coming to check on her and she held her breath and waited. There were no sounds, she had to have imagined them: her nerves and stress getting the better of her. Although the room was in a scattered mess, she didn't want to give up on the possibility of finding something she could use, so she opened a couple more drawers.

Unsurprisingly they too were tossed and untidy but in one, hidden beneath an array of underwear, Sophie found a piece of notepaper with a list of numbers written down. There were two rows of random numbers, would one of these turn out to be the six figure re-coded pin number to unlock the doors?

They had to be!

It was as Sophie hurriedly left the room she heard the first rumble of thunder overhead, so it was likely she didn't have too much time before Lexie came inside, especially if there was torrential rain to go alongside the thunder and lightning.

Just in case Sophie went into her own room and closed the door. If Lexie came down to check on her, the closed-door would-be confirmation she was inside and probably asleep.

She placed the half-full bottle of strong prescription sleeping pills on the top sheet on the bed, alongside the car keys and the list of numbers she collected from the room next door and tried to think what to do next.

She couldn't risk Lexie catching her trying out the numbers on the main door, but she could try the nearest. She snuck out into the hallway and took the top row of scribbled numbers to try the door to the wine cellar. Her logic told her, if one of those lines opened this particular door then it stood to reason the same digits, or one of the other lines, opened the front door and garage. It was her way to escape and get help, because no matter how far she had to go to find a village or town, she would drive all night if she had to, to find a phone or a police station.

She had attempted the top two lines without the welcoming click of release, and although it was initially disappointing, that conundrum could wait. It was hard not to feel hopeful as an idea came to her.

It could work, but she'd have to move quickly. Sophie raced up the stairs to the kitchen, glancing through the open space, making sure Lexie was on the balcony facing the sea so unable to see what she was doing. Stealthily and as quietly as possible Sophie set to work. She had only just finished her task when a figure appeared in the open doorway highlighted by a flash of lightning.

Lexie stepped inside. There was no time to do anything more, except pretend everything was the same, knowing that any sign of a change in her mood might sound alarm bells.

'Oh! I thought you'd be in your room, asleep.' Lexie, with her usual offhand manner, crossed the expanse of the kitchen and opened the large American fridge door. Reaching inside she took a bottle from its innards and took a long thirst-quenching drink of water.

'I did nod off.' Sophie needed more than ever, to appear the same in any response.

'But I think the thunder must have woken me,' Sophie answered, then just to prove her point a loud thunderclap slammed across the sky directly overhead, and rivers of rain crashed down the glass doors.

Lexie didn't comment but sauntered across to a low sofa and threw herself along its length. She sighed, 'Just what I needed in this hell hole, a fucking storm.' she was in a bad mood made worse by the inclement weather.

Sophie, leaning her bottom against a work surface, didn't speak as she watched and waited.

Chapter 14

She couldn't be sure she hadn't overdone the sleeping pills: as much as she'd have liked, she didn't want to kill the woman now in a deep sleep on the sofa.

She had ground up six of the strong tablets and mixed them in the bottle of water, knowing that Lexie would go straight to the fridge and the bottle, to take a long drink when she came in. Sophie thought it would be more than enough to knock Lexie out for a good eight hours. Or that's what she hoped!

She had hoped to locate her phone and charger, she was sure it was hidden somewhere. As quickly as she could she searched for the bag that Lexie always seemed to have with her, maybe her phone was in there. For once there was no sign of the bag, not outside on the balcony, and she might be wrong about that anyway. Now she had the chance, it would be best if she just escaped and got help.

With the list in her hand, she tried the top numbers on the main door's keypad. Once again, the red light blinked back at her, and the door stayed locked. These were not the key codes.

She swore and all but gave up. It was all down to the burgeoning security and safety ethos, but sometimes the rise of pin numbers, key codes, and passwords, and remembering the different combinations. were a bit of a bind. How could she get out without the proper codes to this door and the garage door?

Maybe the codes were written down somewhere in plain sight, a place she'd overlooked? Where did people usually leave notes, shopping lists, appointments or anything that might be needed from day to day? In a kitchen drawer, attached to a fridge by a magnet? Not there. The white fridge door was as pristine and bare as the day it had been installed. Was it more than likely, the list of codes was in that blasted bag of Lexie's? Where had she left it? Her bedroom? She'd have to run down to the lower level and check.

Sophie turned back and was about to descend when something caught her attention. A slight sound? The thunder had rumbled off back out to sea and it appeared the rain had stopped as quickly as it began so had there been a sudden unexplained movement?

Sophie hesitated. Was there someone else in the villa, or once again had she imagined hearing an unfamiliar noise? Had April returned and if she had, how had Sophie missed seeing her? The only room she'd never been inside and had always seemed off limits was the wine cellar so, for whatever reason had April been in there all this time?

Sophie rubbed at her forehead. She was confused and scared.

Cautiously she crept back into the main room and stopped. The sofa, where Lexie had fallen asleep, was now empty. Sophie held her breath, her limbs unable to move to save her.

'It didn't work,' the voice coming from just outside the glass door out on the balcony, now wet after the recent downpour, continued.

'As if you really thought you could get the better of me, Sophie Oxford.'

She sounded self-assured and triumphant even as her adversary took a step onto the balcony.

'Have you forgotten just how much security there is in this place? Did you not think there just might be hidden cameras in the walls?'

Sophie's mind was reeling. She found she was so shocked she couldn't put words together.

Lexie answered for her. 'Obviously not. We have been able to watch you all the time. I watched you spike a bottle of water and decided to play along with your little scheme,' she quickly corrected herself, but this was all part of the game.

'When I say 'we', I mean April and me until— she left us. These are high tech gadgets and the cameras' feed goes straight to monitors, the large one is in the cellar —. Oh I forgot you've never seen inside the wine cellar, have you?' Lexie didn't wait for an answer. She was enjoying herself and mostly revelling in her captive's discomfort.

'April and I are able to watch what you are doing and where you are on our mobile phones. Like the one in my bag,' she lifted up the bag and dangled it close to Sophie's face. How had she missed that? She got the answer.

'I stashed it behind the sunbed out there and you didn't look too hard. Anyway, as I was saying 'Aunty April' took your phone and charger to use to send dear Richard photos of his wife. He had to get the right message across and make sure he realised we meant business.'

'What is this all about?' Sophie was playing for time. 'What exactly is the ship carrying that is worth so much you'll threaten people's lives? My life?'

'Weapons,' Lexie whispered, as if she may be overheard and made a comic face.

'Literally tons and tons of guns and ammo. This load is worth millions to these gangs overseas. Jake is set to make around twenty million from the sale and when we get our thirty percent cut on the deal, well.'

Lexie paused and stepped further onto the balcony. There she spread her arms wide and lifted her face to the sun, now peeking from behind the clouds.

'I love the fresh air, feeling the breeze on my skin. I can't get enough of the sun and the heat.'

She slowly spun her tanned arms outstretched.

'Mmm, that feels good. I'd like to live outdoors all the time; I've had to spend too much of my life locked away inside.'

She didn't expand that statement but stopped and stared once more, letting her words sink into the mind of the woman.

'So I watched you first downstairs searching April's room, then adding a few of her sleeping pills to the bottled water.' She sounded amused by it all.

'I just pretended to get that doped bottle from the fridge and drink from it when I actually picked out the next bottle along. I had you fooled, didn't I? You were too smug, or stupid, to notice.'

She grinned. 'You should see the look on your face. It's a hoot! I wish I had your phone now so I could take a pic and send it to hubby.'

'It's just a game to you, isn't it?' Sophie's heart was racing. What could she do now?

'Did April really leave?' It was a question that had been in her thoughts for a while, she almost didn't want to know the truth and what she suspected had happened to the woman she had thought of as a friend.

'She did go and find a casino, as I told you, but she came back. She started to imagine, a bit like you, that she could start throwing her weight around. April, sweet Aunty April, thought she could get the better of me. Just like you.'

She stopped speaking and her hysterical laughing echoed around the empty villa.

Not for the first time Sophie was convinced she was alone and facing a psychopath.

'April suddenly got cold feet, or grew a conscience or found God, or whatever! She was about to spill the beans and tell you all about our scheme. She had even reached the point of wanting to let you go. Well I had to stop her, didn't I? She sealed her own fate and, just like you will,' Lexie added matter-of-factly, no emotion. 'She had to die.'

Composed and serious once more, she elaborated.

'April had got it into her head that you needed saving —from me. That evening she was going to march into your bedroom and tell you everything, so I had to stop her.'

Sophie felt sick.

'What did you do? Where is she now?'

She didn't say anything for a few minutes as she moved closer to the glass barrier and gazed out towards the horizon, breathing in the strong ozone. It was obvious the mad woman was unconcerned about a possible reaction from Sophie, and supremely confident in her own ability.

'I stabbed her with one of those posh kitchen knives. Now? Right now, her body is locked away in the wine cellar,' she said without any sign of emotion, adding: 'That's probably where you'll be going very shortly.'

Chapter 15

DCI Richard Oxford was really worried.

The information from the FBI, Interpol and other European police sources stating that the huge shipment of obsolete Russian weapons and arms, shortly to arrive on these shores and then brokered on to a middle eastern terrorist group, were now top priority for the major UK security agencies.

Following on from 9\11 and the London bombing, then the recent Iraq war and the downfall of Saddam Hussein, just three years ago, had meant the growth of radical groups and a significant threat.

The world was becoming a very dangerous place fuelled by unscrupulous arms dealers chancing their luck, such as Morgan's Operation Taurus had been set up specifically to intercept and confiscate such a highly prized cargo before it was sold on to these militants. But its success and his wife's safety were now both teetering on a knife edge.

With just thirty-six hours to go before the scheduled arrival of the Zenia, then two days later the Special Ops raid which would ultimately turn out to be a dud, Oxford felt he was on a white-knuckle ride. Any other change of plan by the police and he feared he might never see Sophie again.

With time running out he'd arranged to meet his colleague and the one person he felt he could trust, on a deserted piece of wasteland. He hoped for some good news and some piece of positive intel he could pass on to his superior.

'Sorry I'm late, sir,' having parked up beside the DCI's car the detective inspector sounded out of breath. 'I had to sneak out the back of the station before the Hulk saw me.'

That was the name he'd called DI Elliott Vincent almost from day one. It was a *given* by the team that the two men did not get on.

'He's been nosing around. He knows something's up.'

Richard's grip tightened around the steering wheel.

'Never mind about him,' he said, but silently praying that Vincent wasn't getting too wise to the truth.

Oxford was impatient. 'What have you found out?'

DI Gavin Stevens turned to the notes on his pad, and referred to the folder he'd placed on his lap.

'April Cox, fifty-one and single. She has never married and, with no family to speak of, lives alone in a studio flat on the top floor of that block in Sandwich Lane. In the past she has made a reasonable living from painting landscapes. There was even talk, towards the end of the last century, of her staging an art exhibition in London she was that good, but nothing came of it, and she rarely paints commissions anymore.'

Oxford nodded. That fitted in with the art class scenario.

Stevens continued.

'Cox doesn't have a record as such, but she has a serious gambling addiction which means she owes a lot of money to some unsavoury characters. I'm assuming one of those 'unsavoury characters' is Jake Morgan, sir?'

Oxford nodded but didn't speak. If she owed Morgan, then she might have had no other choice but to go along with Sophie's kidnap.

Gavin Stevens continued.

'I asked around the other flats and the tenants more or less said the same thing. Cox kept to herself, had no real friends. She hasn't been seen for a fortnight and the pile of post and papers pushed through her letter box confirms that.'

The police officer opened the file on his lap and adjusted his reading glasses.

'Now the file on Jake Morgan. He's forty-five. His second marriage to Gemma, fifteen years his junior, was on New Millennium eve. They have two kids, a boy, and a girl.

There are no details of wife number one except a Geraldine Morgan was mentioned at his old address on the '91 census. It's possible she moved abroad after their divorce but there's no way to prove that and it was Gemma Morgan who was named in the more recent 2001 census.

As to Jake he has only a minor police record. When he was nineteen, he was arrested and charged with possession but got off with a fine and since then he appears to have kept his nose clean. He is a well-respected businessman who likes wining and dining with the powerful and elite, including many premier footballers, A-listed film stars and celebs and even our very own member of parliament. It is rumoured he is not opposed to greasing the appropriate palm if he needs to.

Morgan built up his fortune in the eighties and nineties from the booming property market and then turned his attention to betting shops. He acquired about a dozen dotted around the country, but since the brave new world of digital age he sold off the shops and nowadays concentrates on online betting.'

He paused from reading to ask, 'Do you think that could be the connection with April Cox and her gambling?'

Oxford shrugged. He didn't know, nor did he care, but admitted it was very likely that's how the two had crossed paths.

'He owns properties he rents out, here in the UK and in places like Croatia, Poland and Spain. However, during the last couple of years, with the bank crisis and recession, his companies have lost a lot of their value and he's been borrowing heavily to keep afloat. He's been looking for some way to make a fast buck before the banks foreclose.'

Oxford concentrated on an important fact. The original idea was for Sophie to take a seaside painting break with a friend, and the last photo he'd received was of her strolling along a beach. It made sense his wife must be a hostage in one of his holiday homes. Secretly he was dying to go and get Jake Morgan alone and beat the crap out of him, but he knew he couldn't do that.

'Is there a list of his holiday lets in Britain?' he asked.

'There are quite a lot, I would say around the six hundred mark. They cover many of the recognised holiday destinations in places from Cornwall, Wales, Yorkshire up to the highlands of Scotland.

Stevens found another sheath of paper.

'However, I found these dozen or so luxury and top-of-the range coastal properties registered to an offshore company in the Bahamas.'

He handed over the list of converted fisherman's cottage, terraces and villas, and Richard scanned them quickly. Unfortunately, there was no clue to knowing where Sophie was being held. She could be anywhere!

'What do you want me to do next, sir?'

Oxford was thoughtful. He hated having to work virtually on his own, but he had the trusted DI Stevens and the full backing of his senior officer, and for the moment it was best if no one suspected his alternative investigation.

'Right,' he wanted to go over it once more, as much to get it fixed in his own mind as to remind the officer at his side.

'Everything is set for the Operation Taurus raid to be carried out two nights *after* the Zenia docks and unloads her cargo. On the night of the sixth there be no ship and no cargo, and it will appear the team have been given misinformation or incorrect dates. This decision to go with the plan was after my wife's kidnap and Morgan had threatened that if the team didn't play ball and allow the ship to dock unhindered, Sophie would be harmed.'

'And that still stands, sir.'

'Yes, the dangerous shipment of weapons will enter our shores on the fourth and there is nothing we can do about it, unless we can find where my wife is being held and I can get to her in the next twenty-four hours. We know there is an informer on the team, and he must not get a whiff of what you and I are doing, Gavin.'

The officer nodded.

'You secretly keep digging, you might find something, and I'll work on narrowing down the list of holiday lets.' He insisted. 'We must both continue the work as members of Operation Taurus team, so no one grows suspicious. OK?'

'OK.'

Richard Oxford sighed. This covert undercover investigation was proving to be tough, and time was running out.

Chapter 16

Lexie stood facing the hazy horizon, her arms outstretched mimicking the famous scene in the film 'Titanic'.

'Did you see the film? I've watched it again and again?'

She swayed in time with the tune playing out in her head.

'I love all films but especially romances, don't you? My Kyall and me, we are all loved up.'

Lexie, why are you doing this?'

She was slowly turning, her hands above her head, 'flamenco' style.

'I told you. Money, love,' Lexie answered, then as if needing to explain, said.

'From being very young I always wanted what others had and if they didn't hand it over, then I took it. It didn't matter if it was toys or sweets, I just snatched them from some brawling, ungrateful, spoiled brat.'

She was back reliving her past.

'I remember when I was in my teens the girl next door had a brand-new dress. It was very *on trend* and had cost a lot of money and I knew my parents couldn't afford to buy one for me. So I decided if I couldn't have that dress, then neither could — I can't remember her name now. One day I followed her to a bus stop down the road, she was all dolled up in 'my' dress going to meet her boyfriend. She hadn't seen me until it was too late and by then I'd crept up behind her, and using my old man's cigarette lighter, I set fire to the hem of the dress.'

She laughed. It was a hysterical, insane sound.

'It was quite a blaze, I can tell you, and 'what's-her' name screamed enough to wake the dead. I stood and watched; it was *sooo* exciting until people came to see what all the fuss was about. They helped put it out and called for an ambulance.'

Sophie was appalled but an inner voice told her not to react. This was a dangerous and sick woman.

She stayed very still and silent.

Lexie loved an audience, and with an audience of one giving her full attention, she couldn't stop talking.

'She, the girl only had burns on her legs and lower body. She didn't die or anything.'

She rolled her eyes.

'Everyone overreacted, including her parents, and the court thought I should be 'placed in a safe and secure unit' for my own good.'

She sighed, stopped spinning and stood swaying.

'It's always been the same. People don't understand my needs. Nobody has ever given me everything I want. I was married once, ages ago, and he had money, but he didn't think I should spend it. He was another who wanted to keep me a prisoner.'

Sophie wondered what had happened to the unfortunate man, but didn't ask.

'Now I have Kyall. He's lovely. He doesn't begrudge me anything, and when we have all this money — we are going to be married. You know, one of those romantic weddings on an exotic beach.'

She stopped suddenly and her previous faraway look was serious.

'Of course, this all depends on your policeman husband doing as he's told and sticking to the plan. I'll be richer than I have ever imagined, but before that happens there are things to clear up.'

Whether she'd noticed Sophie had taken a step nearer, or was it perhaps the moment before it happened when Lexie realised her ultimate mistake and that she was in the wrong position?

No one would know.

Sophie moved fast, her arms raised without her brain needing to instruct them.

'You're right, Lexie,' she yelled as she pushed her, using all her strength. 'There are things to clear up.'

The other woman tipped backwards over the waist-high glass barrier and Sophie heard Lexie cry out once, then nothing more.

'Oh God! Oh God, I've killed her,' she panicked, repeating it over and over in her head almost afraid to take a breath.

'Oh God, what have I done?'

Nearer to the edge Sophie peered over the rough, rocky, and steep cliff, to the beach six metres down. It wasn't much more than the height of a two-storey building but steep enough to kill or at least break a few bones.

Lexie lay on her back, across two of the protruding boulders which were surrounded by a cluster of smaller rocks.

Her eyes were closed and there could have been blood seeping from the back of her head, but it was the angle of her right leg that told its own story.

Sophie knew she should have checked, but right that moment she didn't care if the mad woman had broken one leg or both and was still alive or not. She had already killed April and Sophie knew, without a shadow of a doubt, she would have been joining her friend in the wine cellar if she hadn't attacked first. She'd face the trauma of what she'd done and any possible charge of manslaughter when this was all over.

Right now, she had to get out of here and get a message to Richard to let him know she was safe. Scooping up Lexie's bag, she ran to the front door hoping and praying that somewhere in the depth of the cluttered bag was the written code numbers to releasing the locks on this and the garage. She still had April's keys and, providing her garaged car was still running, she would be home and dry. And free!

She was breathing so fast, as if she'd run a Marathon, and struggled to stop her hands shaking as she upended the bag, spilling its multiple contents onto the marble floor.

The clatter of bottles of nail varnish and other manicural objects, lipsticks and a small mirror, a tube of hand cream and another of sun cream, a pair of designer sunglasses, the modern MP3 player that had seemed permanently attached to Lexie's ears since her arrival, and a bright, pink-cased mobile phone: the sound echoed loudly around the vast and empty villa.

Chapter 17

There was no list of numbers scribbled on a piece of paper.

Sophie sat down hard on the floor resting her back against the wooden door and surrounded by Lexie's clutter. She picked up the woman's phone but once again, giving Sophie a reason to swear and shout, long and loud, it was locked and could only be opened by a personal pin number. Right that moment she wanted to scream and just give in. The truth was she was locked into what was rapidly turning into her tomb. No one knew she was here and unless she thought logically and fast, she would slowly die.

It seemed so unfair after what she'd been through. She'd survived a brain tumour, and then dying twice on the operating table followed by a course of chemo treatment to eventually be given the all clear, and now she was going to die.

Life really was a bitch at times, but she wasn't beaten yet.

Think! Think!

Would it be possible to climb down to the beach from the balcony? Even if she was able to, without losing her footing and ending up broken on the scattering of rocks below, Lexie's fate, but without a boat to take her along this curving coastline, there was nowhere to go on foot.

To the right were the distant, misty hills and like an optical illusion, there was no way of judging just how close they actually were. She could be walking for hours, or even days, before an unforeseen tide came rushing in or she found other people.

To the left was another barrier of rocks forming a high ridge, from the tall cliff side, stretching far out to sea.

If she was able to get as far as the beach without serious injury, could she risk swimming? She could stay close to the shore, so not out of her depth. Sophie was the first to admit, her swimming acumen was rubbish, and more like a doggy paddle, before she sank. What she would have given for the sight of the speed boat which had been tied up at the jetty just a few days ago?

But getting down to the beach may be her only option and, as she sat there on a chilled floor surrounded by Lexie's handbag clutter, she climbed stiffly to her feet and walked back through the open doors onto the balcony. Overhead the sky remained dull and angry looking, the sun having taken shelter behind a high bank of clouds as the day slowly gave way to an early dusk.

She was reluctant to go to the glass barrier knowing she'd see the woman on the rocks below. Realisation that she had been responsible for her death made her catch her breath.

Clutching the top of a toughened glass panel she stared down.

A greying line of lapping sea edged the sandy beach and the closer, darker shades of rocks stared back at her.

Where was Lexie? What had happened to Lexie?

There had been no tide. In any case it never came up this part of the beach close enough to wash over the rocks and shingle. It couldn't have washed a body out to sea.

Sophie gripped the glass tighter to stop herself fainting. She felt dizzy, disorientated, and sick.

If the woman wasn't where she'd left her, then she couldn't be dead. Sophie had thought she had broken her leg, and she'd seen blood from a head wound.

Or had she just imagined these injuries?

A dreadful idea raced through Sophie's mind. If Lexie's injuries hadn't been as bad as she'd first thought, then it was likely she was on her way, this very second, to finish off what she'd intended because she would know the key code to open the door from the *outside*. Right now, she would be climbing the steep wooden steps, hidden from the balcony on that side by a solid concrete wall, and making straight for the front door.

Sophie had been feeling positive, more hopeful until this moment. A panic attack hovered close to the surface, and she chewed her bottom lip with tension, until she was sure she could taste blood.

Think! Think!

Perhaps she should find some sort of 'weapon' to defend herself? Sophie baulked at a kitchen knife, but if she could locate some other kitchen implement that could disarm Lexie if she appeared still out for blood. A copper pan, coffee grinder? But Sophie quickly dismissed any plan for a fight, brawling was not in her nature.

She'd hide in the cloakroom next to the main door, then if Lexie let herself back in, she could sneak outside behind her back.

Good plan, but what then because without the garage door keycode, she still wouldn't be able to get to April's car. It seemed whatever she considered; Lexie always seemed to have the upper hand.

She had no idea how long she stayed there, her senses were alive to any sounds beyond the closed door, but she was also wasting valuable time. Maybe she would need something to defend herself? Without giving herself time to think, she crept out of the cloakroom and ran to the kitchen. There she grabbed the tall, wooden, and quite weighty, peppermill from the worktop. Holding it like a club she then scooted back to the hall and into the cloakroom, this time making sure to leave the door open just a gap just in case.

Sitting on the only plausible object, Sophie took another look at the list of numbers she'd found in April's room. Was it possible they were specially rearranged like a secret code? Seemed unlikely and anyway this was hardly spies and 007, more 'cops and robbers. Looking again at the numbers, there was a definite familiarity about their arrangement.

They were written like a —!

'Of course, you clot,' she scolded herself in a loud whisper and froze. What if there were people listening in? Sophie laughed at the very idea, then was immediately sombre. How could she tell if there weren't even more secret security and listening devices planted around the place, even in the toilets?

She concentrated once more on the numbers. Lexie had made a point of mentioning April's gambling habit and so it was obvious, apart from the usual gaming tables and casinos, she would probably bet on horse and dog racing and she'd '*do the lottery!*'

Working on that assumption, these were probably no more than April's weekly lotto numbers, jotted down so she'd not forget them. The locking code could be one of these rows of lottery numbers, or randomly chosen numbers or dates or birthdays?

It was possible that April and Lexie had changed the new codes to reflect personal dates and birthdays, which on reflection were of no use in Sophie's current frightening dilemma. They could have been anniversaries, historical, even taken from one or other's cash machine pin numbers. The list was endless – and Sophie did not have the time.

She turned the scrap of notepaper upside down on its side staring, mesmerised but no solution jumped out at her. These particular numbers didn't help —.

Surely the code had to mean something to someone or –?

Or — or? To a few people, or why bother to choose it?

It was a veritable brilliant, lightbulb moment! So her old brain wasn't so addled after all!

Could the choice of the new six number to release the lock, be as simple as that?

Tonight, was when the shipment was due, and presumably the thought of untold riches and a new life rested on its success. Of course, her captors' minds would be focusing on just one date.

The fourth day of August, twenty-0-nine.
482009

Was it really as simple as that?

Only one way to find out.

Very cautiously, with the pepper mill in one hand, raised to counterattack, if need be, Sophie left the cloakroom and moved quickly across the marble floor to the door. Stepping over the upended bag and the tossed items, she carefully tapped in the numbers.

482009.

She figuratively crossed her fingers. If she was wrong about this, then it could be game over and there was no knowing where Lexie was or what she'd be up to next. If she could survive the fall down a mini cliff side, apparently with barely a scratch, then she could pounce as soon as Sophie opened the door.

That was a chance she had to take. First, was it the right set of numbers?

Success! It worked!

The set of six numbers in that order had actually unlocked the door and Sophie held her breath thankful for the positive click. In this luxury property there was no more than a muted, expensive top-of-the-range, coded keypad, door-opening click.

More cautious than ever she opened the door just the smallest of gaps and gulped in air as if she'd been suffocating inside.

Freedom. Of sorts. Felt good!

She filled her lungs, tasting salt and ozone in the stiff breeze blowing inland from the sea.

There was no sudden attack, no resistance so she stepped outside the confines of her 'prison' and glanced quickly around. There was no sign of life, either in the side courtyard leading to the garage and the driveway to the front of the villa, or the area to her right leading to the steps to the lower beach. She tried not to think of a seriously injured Lexie, maybe bleeding and lying very close by, she had threatened to kill Sophie.

What now?

With the pepper mill clutched in one hand she ran over to her only viable option if she was to get away. Would she be lucky and find it was the same six digits to open the garage's key lock?

Chapter 18

'What have you got?'

DI Gavin Stevens had had to call in favours from other police departments as well as more unorthodox methods to persuade the tech team to get this piece of information, and he was unsure if Oxford would have approved. But then again, the DCI's wife was in great danger and time was running out, so the officer should probably be applauded and not reprimanded.

They had arranged the meeting in an empty pub car park outside of Thornhill and, as Steven's climbed into Oxford's passenger seat, both men glanced nervously around. The two cars were the only vehicles in sight, but there was always the chance one or other might have been followed if 'the person of interest' had grown suspicious.

Once again Stevens adjusted his specs on his thin nose and opened the cardboard box file on his lap. It was an ongoing joke within their own team that, while every other officer on the force now used modern mobiles and/or computers to log in and download all info into files and documents, Stevens still preferred the written, or in this case, printed word.

'Sir, I've discovered more about the first Mrs Morgan,' he paused, aware Oxford would suspect the discovery wasn't necessarily 'by the book', and a nifty bit of hacking had gone on into files sealed by the Courts.

'Course, this wasn't obtained through the official channels,' he thought he needed to explain before continuing.

He needn't have worried. Richard assured him: 'Unfortunately Gavin, nothing about this situation is based on the norm, but 'needs must'. I'm convinced they'll be holding her somewhere very isolated, far enough away from crowded holiday areas and people, so as not to attract unwanted attention. I'm literally clutching at straws and, if by finding the whereabouts of the first wife, she just might know of a likely place to keep their prisoner.'

He rubbed a shaking hand across his forehead. 'That's if it's somewhere along the coast and they haven't moved her or already done something —.'

He sounded at the end of his tether and, not for the first time, Gavin wondered if the chief inspector should have been taken off this case right at the start?

'I have to try anything and everything,' he added.

'Sir,' Stevens accepted this. He had only met the boss's wife on two occasions, but he liked her. When she'd been diagnosed with a brain tumour, he'd been the first to offer hope. He wanted to do that now and do all he could, no matter how questionable their actions.

'The first wife Geraldine has quite an interesting history, by all accounts.' he read from the notes.

'She was born 1980 in the seaside town of Northport and the first child of Sally and Joe Kelly. The couple had another child, a boy Lucas who died in tragic circumstances when he was three. Geraldine was *trouble* from the word go, with what these days would be given any number of abbreviations and acronyms used to diagnose her particular problems. From being a toddler and, more than once, the Kelly's' neighbours called the police when a sudden tantrum meant she was screaming for hours on end. This could have been caused by something as simple as being told to eat her food or after being told to give her brother back some item she'd snatched away from him. It was initially diagnosed as ADHD, but it turned out to be far more serious.

Geraldine was five when Sally Kelly left the children playing together in the sitting room while she was outside hanging the washing. She ran back inside when Geraldine started on one of her screaming fits and found the boy, Lucas, lying on the floor with a head injury. His sister insisted he'd fallen and bumped his head against the edge of the table. He died the next day and at first it was deemed to be a tragic accident.

Geraldine was asked about the accident and the police liaison and family officer had to be extra careful with a child that age. Yet even at five she never changed her statement repeating she didn't know how her brother had come by the suspicious bruising around his neck and upper arms.

Eventually an analyst measured the finger marks and compared these with the girl's hand size and confirmed there was no doubt they'd been made by a child's hands. Their conclusion was Lucas had been held and thrown against, or pushed deliberately onto the table's edge. However, it was a controversial and highly charged argument about the age of the suspect and one expert questioned the timing of the bruises and when they could have occurred. With one argument cancelling out another, at the inquest the coroner verdict: death by misadventure.

It was noted by a few of the people connected with the Kelly family that the sister Geraldine never mentioned Lucas again and, if his name ever came up in conversation and was within her hearing, for years after she would have a dramatic screaming fit. Nothing could be proven against her, and now their only child, they spoiled her rotten. The Kelly's were a hard-working couple, not much money to spare for expensive toys and treats, so it was often impossible to keep her happy. That didn't matter as far as the girl was concerned, whatever Geraldine wanted she must have, no matter the cost.

There are a number of instances where she reportedly stole from her classmates and other pupils and along with the inevitable fits of screaming to get her own way, this went on into her teens.

It came to a head when, at ten years old, she tried to stab a classmate with the point of a biro because he wouldn't hand over his pocket money. It was then that both the school and child psychologists were in agreement she needed special care, but Mr and Mrs Kelly were having none of it. They insisted their daughter was just high-spirited and had been play-acting, having watched a film on the TV, and although she'd drawn blood Geraldine hadn't meant the boy any real harm, it was hardly more than a minor scratch on his neck.'

DI Steven's stopped reading, to take a breath and turn the page.

Richard wasn't sure whether this information would be of any use in tracing Sophie in the next hours, already he could sense that Morgan had won the battle to get his shipment in dock without any interference. After all, he and Steven could be barking up the proverbial wrong tree and wasting time. However, from what he 'd heard so far, the first wife of Mason's did sound an intriguing subject.

The inspector continued his narrative.

'Geraldine Kelly left school with only average grades and worked in a number of low paid jobs, including an estate agency, bar work and shop assistant. She left each of the jobs after a short time saying she either didn't like the work, it was boring, she didn't get paid enough to get out of bed in the mornings and a host of excuses. More often than not she was fired for laziness, and/or rudeness to the customers.'

Steven turned the page.

'It was in the summer of 1996 when there was quite a serious incident that meant Geraldine Kelly was institutionalised for the first time'.

DCI listened closely. He was interested in this person, however still wondering how this information equated to his missing wife.

'It was over another girl's dress,' Stevens said. 'Geraldine wanted one the same and when she didn't get it, she set the garment on fire with the girl still wearing it.'

Richard whistled through his teeth.

'Oh my God. If Geraldine Kelly is really April Cox and she's a sociopath. Does she have Sophie?'

'It's not April Cox, sir.' Gavin continued reading from his notes.

'It was a few years after Kelly was released from the secure unit, she changed her appearance and her name and as Lexie Price she met Jake Morgan. She was nineteen and Morgan was fifteen years older, but the couple married only weeks after their first meeting.

I think it was doomed from the start, and their marriage didn't last more than six months. Jake by then was an up-and-coming highflyer in the business world and set to go far, but found his new bride capricious and demanding, and her unpredictable mood swings meant she didn't fit in with his future image. He couldn't control her, and she was a serious flirt. Even on their honeymoon she had an affair with another man and when she started sleeping with one of his colleagues he'd known for years, Kyall Clarke, it seems Jake openly encouraged their illicit relationship. Their marriage ended with an annulment and Lexie getting a reasonable divorce settlement. Only a day after the Decree Absolute Lexie and Clarke moved in together and they've lived together ever since.'

'I'm not sure that helps with tracking down where they're keeping Sophie and time is running out,' Richard's nerves were on edge. It was lunchtime, it was August the fourth and there was less than twelve hours to go before the Zenia docked. It didn't help his frustration and growing dread, not being able to seek out a possible hostage location.

He sighed.

'All right Gavin, we have so little to go on, but see what else you can come up with. In the meantime, I have to lie and keep up the pretence to the whole of the Operation Taurus team and tell them that, although the plans have changed, we'll still achieve our goal on the 6th. The only thing that will change that is if I find my wife in the next few hours.'

Chapter 19

'I've found something, sir,'

Eighty-three minutes later DI Stevens burst into the room without the necessary and customary knock of the door. He couldn't wait to pass on his findings. This was too important, and he'd expected to found DCI Oxford alone in his office, but instead he was seated next to SIO Jim Telford who was explaining something highlighted on the computer screen

'What is it, Steven?' Telford snapped and glanced up, unable to hide his irritation. He was explaining, to his second-in-demand, an important detail regarding the forthcoming operation and he hated to be interrupted whatever the urgency: this officer in particular could annoy him just by being in the same room.

'Oh, sorry sir. I was checking on something for DCI Oxford, but it's not important.'

'Well, tell him or show him, but make it quick,' Telford yelled. He was in charge, and he liked the team to remember that fact, but just as sudden his attitude charged. He also wanted the next couple of days to run as smoothly, and problem free, as possible.

'Never mind,' he stood and made for the door. 'I think we've covered everything Richard.'

He'd been going over with the detective chief inspector for the umpteenth time, the alternative sixth of August covert raid at the port. He was insistent that was the only chance to save his wife.

Earlier he'd repeated again: 'Only you and I know about the change and, until Sophie is safe and sound, we have to stick with it.'

He'd seemed unconcerned that the team, his team, were being kept in the dark, and just in case the worried husband hadn't quite understood the seriousness, he'd added.

'As soon as Morgan and his gang have the ship's cargo in their possession tonight, without any interference, his go-between has promised Sophie will be released. At that point I will give orders to arrest Jake Morgan, Clarke and the rest of the gang and confiscate the illegal contraband.

Just remember, as far as the Operation Taurus team is concerned the ship was held up for two days in the Channel. The truth will come out eventually but by then you will have your wife back.'

Now he left the office with an air of confidence and stopped to have a word and a laugh with DI Vincent who was leaning against the water dispenser, ogling a junior female officer walking past.

'Sorry, sir,' without being told to, DI Gavin Stevens closed the door and sat on the edge of the chair across the desk from Oxford.

The inspector brushed this aside with a flick of his hand. He didn't altogether agree with the way this operation was going, but he was more concerned about his missing wife than officer protocol or to pursue any further objections. He was still hopeful Operation Taurus would come right in the end.

Keeping his doubts and thoughts to himself he said: 'OK Gavin, what have you found?'

The younger DI was flushed with enthusiasm. 'I've been looking at some of the coastal properties owned by Morgan or one of his property companies. I dismissed any situated in busy towns or where there would be a lot of tourists at this time of the year and concentrated only on holiday properties built in isolated areas with little or no public access. With the help of Google Maps, I first picked out three that might just fit the bill.'

He pulled out a print of an enlarged area of the west coast. He'd circled potential sites but one in particular required an extra cross at the side.

'I've eliminated the fisherman's terraced cottage, it's isolated but also has potential for curious neighbours.

The second, a holiday bungalow seemed more likely but then on closer investigation it's close to a busy road and a farmhouse, so any unusual activity could make the farmer suspicious. The last thing one would want if you have a hostage locked up on your property, is nosy neighbours.'

He paused just long enough for a reaction, but when Oxford remained still and silent, he continued.

'I think this could be the place they are holding Mrs Oxford.'

He pointed to the crescent shaped piece of coastline.

Jake Morgan Holdings bought this part of the coast because of its isolation. The modern villa was built into a rocky outcrop two years ago, originally as a holiday home for the Morgan family. It was expensively kitted out with all mod cons, a wine cellar, a state-of-the-art security system, all high tech. From the accounts of a few locals, wife Gemma Morgan didn't take to it complaining it was too far away from shops and civilization. The family only stayed there for one week and the local police were called to a noisy drink and drugs-fuelled orgy after the villa was rented out for Christmas and New Year. Since then, it has hardly been in use. The only way to get to it is by boat, or a single back road from the closest village.'

Richard was interested yet cautious, so much relied on this being right.

'So you think this just might be the place? Show me on Google Maps. Can we zoom in closer to the area?'

He concentrated on the aerial map on the screen.

'It certainly seems isolated. The property is fronting the crescent shaped beach and that —,' he stared as close as he could,' That could be the wooden structure, like a mini jetty a portion could be seen in that last photo of Sophie walking on a beach.'

He couldn't bear it if he was to get his hopes up and fail at the last moment.

He stood, grabbing his mobile and car keys.

'I've got to assume this is the place they are holding my wife.'

He glanced at his watch.

'Send the coordinates to my phone. It's actually closer than I imagined it to be, so about a three hour drive up the coast.'

DI Stevens wasn't so sure.

'You can't go on your own, sir. There's no knowing how many you might find when you get there and without back-up –.'

Even as he was objecting, he could tell from Oxford's face he wasn't going to change his mind.

'I have to go and get her out of there and I have to do this on my own. Meanwhile you 'hold the fort,' tell Telford I'm — oh I don't know. If he asks, tell him I'm so worried about my wife I've taken a break, but I'll be back with the team if there is any good news before this evening. Try not give away the fact you know what is going on – or give away where I'm really off too'

He paused.

His urgency was making him gabble, but he knew Gavin would get the main drift of his orders.

Without a word to the others seated and chatting idly around the main briefing room. It seemed with time on their hands, now the raid was cancelled at least for two days, there was very little left to do.

DCI Richard Oxford rushed out of the station and to his car.

Chapter 20

It was too much to ask that the same six numbers would open the garage door.

Sophie had rushed to the top of the wooden steps down to the beach. She half expected to find Lexie crouching there, someone possibly injured from a twenty plus foot drop, was hardly likely to walk away unscathed. Yet, apart from what may have been blood smeared across the rock where presumably she'd hit her head, there had been no sign of the killer anywhere. Was it possible she had got up and simply walked away? Seemed highly unlikely, but not knowing the answers left Sophie feeling very wary and vulnerable. Lexie could be anywhere, waiting to make her next move.

Trying not to glance to her right or left, she ran to the garage door praying she'd be able to open the door. She had April's car keys in her pocket and, still clutching the pepper mill in her left hand, she typed the same six numbers into the keypad.

Nothing happened. There wasn't the gentle click which had opened the main door and she'd expected to slowly lift the up-and-over mechanism.

Sophie tried again, this time carefully taking her time in case the first try, she'd mistakenly entered the wrong number.

482009.

The garage door stayed stubbornly shut.

In the ten days since she'd been there, she'd only needed to open the villa door to let herself back inside, on the odd occasion April was on the beach. Up to now she'd had no reason to try the other locked doors on the property and they had remained firmly shut. It had been too much of a hope that the same code would open them all.

Sophie was frustrated and kicked out in anger and frustration at the gleaming paintwork, stubbing her sandal clad toe in the process.

She stood for a couple of minutes unsure what to do next and deeply disappointed that her seemingly one avenue of escape, sat on the other side of the door.

What to do now? She was stranded far from any town or village. April had told her they would not be disturbed by locals, or suddenly invaded by other holiday makers as the nearest town was miles away and the villa, and the beach, were private property.

It was beginning to rain just to add to her misery. Not a sudden cooling downpour but a gentle mist which, inevitably, seemed to soak through to the skin. The low, grey clouds matched her mood to perfection.

There was no other option, she would have to start walking along the long private road and hopefully, eventually, find herself on a public road. Sophie wished she could recall more about their journey here. How long the journey or places she would have passed through was vague, as if she'd been asleep through most of the miles.

She looked down at her feet, hardly noticing the broken toenail. Her rubber flip-flops were hardly adequate, but she couldn't go back inside that place to collect any of her things, not at the risk of coming face to face with the psychopath Lexie. She had to get away and get help.

It was quite a narrow, natural sandy driveway along the side to the front, hardly wide enough for a vehicle to the garage. It was wedged between the tall banks of gorse and bracken that knit tightly together to hold the sand dune in place and the steep concrete villa wall opposite.

Once passed the property the path gave way to a slightly wider road, bordered on both sides by more overgrown natural hedges and tall windswept trees. If she could get to the main road and flag down a passing motorist?

Sophie felt very alone and vulnerable as she set off at a steady pace wary of any slight movement or sound. Her inadequate sandals flopped against the unmade road surface and the drizzle soaked through her cotton t-shirt. She wished she could run, take to her heels and sprint to safety.

A car was coming fast heading in her direction, its headlights like two piercing yellow eyes cutting through the greyness.

Should she wave it to stop, ask for help? But on this road how could she know whether the driver was friend or foe? Like a rabbit in the headlight Sophie stopped, unable to move a step as the car got closer. Was it about to run her down? Her limbs were refusing to cooperate to jump out of the way.

The vehicle sped closer until it came to an abrupt stop only yards from the terrified woman.

Sophie felt the world spin and the ground tilt as she first recognised the familiar Lexus and then, through the windscreen, its driver.

Once in the safety of Richard's car, Sophie found she couldn't stop crying. The trauma of the last few days, the stress and now, the relief at seeing her husband's car with his anxious face staring back at her through the rain-washed windscreen, had been just too much.

He'd already held her close and, although it wasn't cold, had wrapped a car rug he found in the boot, around her shaking shoulders.

'Richard, I think I killed her.'

This was all he'd got out of Sophie since he'd come across the bedraggled figure scurrying along the empty road.

'Don't think about her right now,' he tried to reassure his wife. 'You're safe and that's all that matters.'

As he'd headed towards home she'd stared, without blinking and a sure sign of shock, at the road ahead as he drove through the rain. The rhythm of the windscreen wipers was almost mesmeric and calming.

And he'd tried to calm her down while at the same time making a very important call on his car radio. He hoped to be part of the events that evening now they would go ahead with the raid at the docks, but making sure his wife was checked over at the hospital was paramount, as was sending the local force plus a CSI team to secure the villa as soon as possible.

'We'll get you checked over and then a nice cup of tea and perhaps some food —.'

The mood in the car lightened a whole lot

more when Richard, glancing at the forgotten object still clutched tightly in her fist, added:

'But honestly Soph, you didn't need to provide the pepper.'

Chapter 21

Three days later:

Sophie was finally back home having spent time in hospital being checked over after her ordeal.

'No problems.'

Had been her specialist's verdict.

'We've done all the tests and the only difference is a residue of Temazepam left in your system.'

'I was very lethargic from day one,' she told Richard. 'I think when we stopped for a break and I nipped to the Ladies, April spiked my coffee. She then took a scenic route, possibly doubling back so it seemed further and more isolated than it really was '

Her husband agreed. 'The whole time you were being held as a hostage you were given a regular dose of sleeping pills in your food and drink, so you were constantly disoriented and confused.

Her compulsive gambling habit meant she owed a lot of people a lot of money and it was Jake Morgan, having been told by an informant that the authorities knew all about the major shipment due in August, he hatched a plan to kidnap you and use you as a bargaining tool. He offered to clear Cox's debts if she played her part.'

'And I really thought April was a friend,' she was angry at the deception but also sad after her murder had been confirmed when the police had broken the door into the wine cellar. They had found April Cox's body just as her killer had described.

'Quite a surprising space and not just filled with wine racks and crates of booze,' explained the officer in charge. 'There was a mini command centre with a split screen monitor showing the images from the different cameras hidden inside, and the ones along the perimeter of the property. The owner was really into top class security systems. We found the body of a woman with a kitchen knife in the back. The doctor confirmed it had pierced the heart and she would have died almost immediately.'

'Jake Morgan's plan was to keep you shut away, but safe, and as long as Operation Taurus was cancelled, it was working out as he'd hoped.'

'But I was never going to be freed?' Sophie whispered.

For a moment Richard wondered about giving his wife the true answer. But then again this was Sophie and during their married life he'd never been able to lie without her knowing.

'CSI found your mobile and charger on the monitor table in the wine cellar. As long as they needed to send me videos from your phone, to prove you were still alive, then you were safe. By the way, I truly believe April was not part of that and when she discovered the truth and that you were to die, she was all set to get you out of there. Lexie Price discovered what she was intending so killed her.'

'I thought I'd killed Lexie when I pushed her off the balcony.'

He was quick to reassure her.

'She was temporarily knocked out from the fall and had suffered a deep cut on her leg and concussion, but it was mainly her wounded pride, that someone should finally fight back, which hurt her most.'

Her husband smiled reassuringly.

'When she finally decided to talk, she said she'd *fallen* off the balcony and when she came round, battered, and bruised and dazed, realising the gang's hostage would be trying to escape she considered going after you. Lexie didn't think she'd be able to climb the steps back to the villa to retrieve her phone and the only option was April's car in the garage, but in any case, she couldn't have driven away because she didn't have the keys.

Somehow, unsure what to do Lexie, managed to stumble along the sand to that outcrop of rocks that had formed across the beach from the land to the sea. It's hidden by the villa's wall on that side, so that was the reason you didn't see her when you looked over the balcony.'

Richard paused making sure Sophie, still in her fragile state, was keeping up with his narrative.

'She wasn't that hurt or confused not to see she had to act quickly and get a message to Morgan that their hostage was now loose. Lexie knew the other side of that pile of rocks was a small fishing community and if she could climb over, she could find a phone and text, or ring, her boyfriend Kyall Clarke. She'd almost made it but when she dropped down to the beach on the other side, she must have passed out again and was found by a man walking his dog. He rang the police and ambulance services.'

'I had no idea I was that close to other people. They told me the villa was miles away from towns or villages —.'

He took his wife's hand. 'Don't worry love, it's over. Lexie Price has been charged with the murder of April Cox so is no more of a threat. Alongside her boyfriend Clarke and his boss Morgan she is also charged with kidnap and false imprisonment —and a whole list of other crimes. The list keeps growing.'

Chapter 22

Epilogue

Chief Inspector Richard Oxford had been summoned and it felt not unlike an errant pupil sent to the Head's office for detention, except nothing could be farther from the truth.

It was police headquarters and the ACC; Assistant Chief Constable Rainer shook his hand then offered him a seat.

'So, Oxford, the ship and its infamous cargo has been impounded, the captain and crew detained? Importantly Jake Morgan and the other members of his team have been arrested and charged with a number of offences, am I right?'

'Sir.'

'Operation Taurus was an outstanding success, a good job done, and case closed — except for their trials coming up in the near future, eh?'

Richard nodded.

'I have to say that kidnapping your wife was a rum deal, and it took some nerve to escape the way she did. I take it she's recovered from her ordeal?'

'She has, thank you sir. We decided we both need a holiday, after all that has happened, so we fly out to America to spend the rest of the summer with her family.'

'Good for you. Well, give your dear wife my kind wishes, she's a brave woman.'

'It was a good thing to put me in the picture with your suspicions and how your poor wife was being held hostage. I'm not sure I'd have agreed to you shooting off like that on your own, after you got a lead to her whereabouts.'

He allowed a smile to lift the corners of his mouth.

'However,' he continued. 'Once you phoned directly to my private line, to say she was safe then I was able to continue Operation Taurus and set the wheels in motion, so to speak. All in all, it was an excellent night for results, and we should all be pleased.'

Rainer sat back against the plush leather chair and unconsciously straightened the line of his jacket uniform. He didn't wait for a response before saying with a sense of built-up anger and an air of serious authority.

'It goes without saying that one of our number is a disgrace to the force,' he tilted the chair back so he could stare at the outdated moulded pattern on the ceiling.

'You already had information that there was a bent copper keeping Morgan informed on everything the team was up to, regarding the intended raid on the port. When did you first get a clue to who it was?'

'At first I was on the wrong track. I'd thought it was another DI, mouthy, opinionated and always ready with objections, so my thoughts did go in the direction of Elliott Vincent. He proved me wrong, and I have to say he played a blinder that evening when, somewhat foolishly and after he'd been wounded in the arm, he singlehanded disarmed that villain with the handgun.'

'Mmm, I know who you're talking about. He's up for a commendation.'

'I think I knew who the bent copper was,' said Oxford.

'It was during the first team briefing by SIO Jim Telford. He kept making silly mistakes then having to correct himself, like saying the intended shipment was due in port on the sixth of August then quickly correcting it to the fourth as if his mind was in two places. When asked by one of the team, he said the value of this illicit cargo was about eleven million euro when I knew it was worth three times that amount, almost as if he wanted to understate the seriousness of the crime.'

'So what decided it?'

'I'd received that message and the first pictures of my wife during that briefing and immediately after it finished, I showed the message to Telford. It was almost as if he didn't have to think about it, as if the plan to rearrange the date to go along with Morgan's shipment had been thought out beforehand. It was as if the SIO had had prior knowledge of the kidnapping and he'd previously worked out the alternative plan with Morgan.'

'It all fitted, eh?'

'Yes sir. Jim Telford had been approached by Jake Morgan with an offer he couldn't refuse just after the scheme to import illegal weapons, then sell them on to a terrorist group, first materialised. Telford was getting ready for retirement, and he decided his pension needed topping up, so Morgan offered him a six-figure sum if he kept him informed of everything, and he'd get paid after the job was done.'

'Telford's been detained on corruption charges and will be charged, I take it?'

'Yes sir. He was arrested at the port just after the Zenia docked and the Armed Response rounded up the gang, he realised then he'd been tricked and with nowhere to go went quietly.

On the other hand, Jake Morgan wasn't at the port to watch the unloading. He'd left all that to Kyall Clarke and the rest, as an influential businessman he was never one to get his hands dirty. He was later arrested at his house while watching TV with his family.'

Rainer nodded with satisfaction. He regretted Telford's hand in this unpleasant episode, but the main thing was the cargo would be taken somewhere and destroyed.

'Very well, Oxford. Well done to everyone involved.'

He lowered his voice as if suddenly the walls had ears.

'Now these are worrying times, both here and abroad. We mustn't forget the terrorist bombings in the States and then a couple of years ago, the London bombings, so this whole situation needs to be kept under wraps or it could cause panic — you get where I'm coming from?'

'Yes sir.'

'As you were, Richard –.'

The sudden use of his first name didn't go unnoticed by the officer. 'This file is to go into the Top-Secret drawer for now. Maybe one day, in the future when this world is a safer place then it can become public knowledge, but for now—.'

Rainer actually touched the side of his nose as a further sign of absolute secrecy.

He relaxed again and rested his hands across his stomach.

'So that's that, then.' He waited until the officer was at the door before adding a cheerful, 'Bon voyage, Chief Inspector. Enjoy your trip.'…

www.ingramcontent.com/pod-product-compliance
Lightning Source LLC
Chambersburg PA
CBHW052005150726
47999CB00004B/1529